Camille C

Promising accountant Lacy Pondwater never wanted to own the Mistletoe Motel. However, when Lacy's mother passes away and her dad grows too old to readjust roof tiles, she scrambles, with the help of her younger sister Stacy, to keep the family business afloat. Worse, still the motel has been in desperate need of an update since the '80s and is overlooked by travelers thanks to GPS maps routing away potential customers. On a constantly shrinking shoestring budget, Lacy maxed out every credit card and is at the end of her rope.

After a few too many glasses of wine and paranormal crime shows, Lacy embellishes the description of the Mistletoe Motel online to include Victorian era haunts and the occasional ghost encounter. Business rapidly picks up and after a few days, Stacy tells Lacy that guests have been finding their belongings in the strangest of places, like inside of the chimney. A question slowly circles in the back of Lacy's mind. Did she inadvertently invite a haunting to Mistletoe Motel, or are her eager guests merely manifesting their own adventures? Of course, white lies always come back to bite, and when a ghost hunting television show asks to film, the sisters reluctantly agree. Only a Christmas miracle can save the motel from bankruptcy and Lacy from a life of fraud.

The Mystery of Mistletoe Motel. Copyright © 2021
Camille Cabrera.

This is a work of fiction. The characters and events in
this book are fiction and from the author's imagination.
Any resemblance to actual persons, living or dead,
locales or events is completely coincidental.

for motivating the birth of this story. May we all have
the courage to find and accept love.

"Dang it!" The expletive rolled from my tongue as steam nearly poured from my ears. My temper was about to erupt. The only thing holding back my verbal eruption of epic proportions was the tiniest bit of patience that I'd haphazardly taped back together, just like every single pipe and banister inside of our crumbling motel.

Stacy was so busted. How many times had I told her to make sure the meat locker was closed? How many times had I politely opened and closed it in front of her doe-eyed stare in the hopes that at least one lightbulb would turn on in that willfully empty house of a brain? Too many. Now, she was so dead. Well, more figuratively than literally. She was my younger sister, after all.

Of course, I knew that I wasn't being fair. Stacy had a great heart with a wonderfully vibrant open mind, but sometimes her attempts at helpfulness really made it difficult to keep the motel afloat. Her real calling was instructing yoga classes in an outdoor setting surrounded by vibrant people and my real calling was hiding behind piles of papers dotted with tiny numbers.

the legacy that our parents had left us. It felt like I'd mentally carved out a room in my mind for accounting and simply got up and left the next day. I hadn't even settled into the role for a full day before saving the family business rightly took priority. Maybe once everything has settled I could one day follow along as Stacy teaches a yoga class. Until then, we were stuck working together with tensions beyond high and stress levels operating at maximum capacity.

We weren't always like this. I shook away the thoughts from another time and snapped back to the moment. A new fresh wave of anxiety masked as fear zipped through my bloodstream.

I could just picture Stacy's slim arms folded over her chest as her statuesque features turned shocked and tinged with embarrassment. I angrily stomped around the piles of ruined meat products. The gene pool had played the opposite card with me. It had graciously provided me with all of the potential to be an excellent accountant as well as all of the love of pastries to also be in competition with the Pillsbury Doughboy. At least, that's how I felt living through my early teens and my youth, but nearly a decade later, it now meant that I enjoyed my little dimples and curves in a way that younger me would take ten years to fully understand.

The slight stench told me the meat was bad, but that didn't stop the dreamer in me from personally inspecting every single thawed rib-eye by hand.

The earliest risers in the motel were about to get up and the Mistletoe Motel had no viable meat options for our widely broadcasted continental breakfast. It was a tradition from our parents that Stacy and I had yet to throw away. No matter how costly. Sentiments were expensive.

In all honesty, we only had a single room booked and that was still more than our usual occupancy rate. The real problem was that we no longer had any meat for ourselves or any future potential guests. A girl could dream of the latter.

Worse still, we had no viable meat for breakfast, lunch, or dinner for the next week. That was a more realistic hurdle. I rubbed my face in agitation as my messy mop of brown hair remained barely restrained by a threadbare hairband. I ran my tongue over my slightly college, but that was no longer in the cards for now. The bottom teeth were pushed together like a hungry shark. The dentist had said that the enamel would likely slowly erode if left untreated. I had laughed until tears had threatened to fall at the literal metaphor for the state of the motel that now resided on the inside of my mouth. It was a visible fixer-upper and a ticking time bomb of repercussions that was just waiting to explode.

Not that I minded. Well, maybe I did care and that's why this meat-locker-gate was just the perfect excuse to release some steam.

Two flights of well-worn cream carpeted stairs later and I huffed, hunched over, directly outside of Stacy's room. My long fingers rapped against the wooden door as I called, "Stacy, get up, you murderer! The meat locker was left open and everything inside has gone bad. I need to go shopping for food. Please watch the front desk!"

Two sets of voices muttered from behind the door. One was distinctly irritated and feminine, and the other was much deeper. After a few seconds, Stacy

Her eyes quickly widened in alarm once she processed my words. She groaned, "I could have sworn it was closed!"

She leaned against the doorframe and tried her best puppy dog eyes as she added, "It's still really early in the morning. I'm sure that no one would notice if we slept in for another hour."

My blank stare brokered no arguments so she sighed, "Fine, let me just throw on some clothes."

I nodded in agreement and slumped back against the heavily stuccoed walls. It prickled against my skin and became a physical reminder of the growing list of updates that needed to be done in order to bring the motel into the 21st century. Baby steps.

While I waited, my mind drifted a few years into the past. The place had definitely seen better days. Our parents had bought this Victorian mansion and every detail had been painfully renovated during the 80s, which honestly was not a great decade for updates if the salmon colored backsplash tiles in the bathrooms were anything to go by.

with eager tourists and curious sightseers. Weary travelers who had needed a place to rest their head a few paces away from the main road had entered the front door like clockwork.

Now, thanks to GPS and a new toll highway, the occasional visitor was rare and the clientele were much less than family oriented. Roughnecks and bottle lovers tended to stick together.

Unfortunately, the motel wasn't updated enough to interest a different clientele. The days of family vacationers were long gone. Now, we used every cut, corner, and tax break in the book just to keep this metaphorical ship from sinking. Family legacy and all.

"I'm here, I'm here. Let's see what we can do." Stacy's hourglass figure slipped around the doorframe as her vibrant, blonde hair whirled around to her hips. The naturally light color emphasized her almost ocean-colored gaze. She was the exact physical opposite of me. Apparently, our personalities had also manifested as polar opposites. As our father had loved to say, we were two sides of the same coin.

stood out against his dark skin. I averted my gaze to the wall above the door. I tried to give him some privacy as his flustered hands quickly worked over the cotton material. It wasn't much of a surprise that Jeffrey and Stacy were together. They both maintained the same exact peaceful temperament in even the most unpleasant situations. Always cool and casual with a hint of new-age.

My eyes explored the stuccoed wall as though it were the most interesting thing in the world. After all, technically being his boss sometimes made it difficult to navigate our multilayered work environment. Not that the technicality of employment really mattered. Jeffrey was part of our quickly condensed family and had helped us keep the motel together for almost three years.

"Good morning, Lacy." Jeffrey grumbled, in his usual deep baritone. He blocked the length of the doorway with his broad shoulders. His impressive height hovered just about an inch below the top of the doorframe. Jeffrey's heart of gold was wrapped and sealed within the body of a football star.

I didn't bother speaking about the obvious shenanigans. No point in drawing out and dissecting their night. At 20 years old, Stacy was definitely an adult, even if she didn't like to behave like one most of the time. Hence, the meat locker. She was a free spirit just like our mother.

Jeff stifled a yawn as he garbled out, "Not at all. I suppose it's about time we get started with the day."

I nudged my head to the right and they both followed down the shallow-stepped multi-leveled spiral staircase all the way down to the ground floor. Tendrils of early morning light promised a sunnier than normal October morning. The tendrils of sun bounced off the smattered layer of snow that would soon melt away during the height of the afternoon heat.

"Right, I should be back in an hour with more food. Call me if something happens, even though I doubt anything will. I'm sure you both know that we only have room number one occupied. It's occupied by Mister Handsy, but still, it's the principal. One bad online review and we're done."

Jeffrey only likes to feed our guests brisket for breakfast."

She playfully bumped her hip against Jeffrey's thigh due to their height difference. Jeffrey feigned hurt and placed a hand against his heart. "I will have both of you good ladies know that some people enjoy flavor and substance for their meals. Who am I to starve out hard-paying guests?"

"Guest," Lacy teasingly quipped.

Jeffrey simply shrugged his shoulders and ambled in the direction of the kitchen. He drawled, "I'll clean it out. Stacy can put some sage in there to ward off the bad spirits."

"Why stop at the meat locker? Let's just sage the whole place. At this point, it could only help."

"Really, Stacy?" I groaned against the back of my hand as my sister childishly stuck out her tongue.

Stacy countered, "Cleansing a space isn't a joke. Both of you really just don't understand the importance of good energy."

starting from bankruptcy."

Stacy rolled her eyes at me as she plopped down into the bar-height chair behind the front desk. It wasn't much of a front desk. The desk was more like a music stand that we had found at a garage sale a few months ago and repurposed. The original desk split in two when Jeffrey had leaned against it.

After that, Stacy had spent two days assuring him that it wasn't his fault. It really wasn't. The desk had only two stable legs. It was only a matter of time before it broke into smithereens. The furniture designer had probably never accounted for the weight of a 350-pound man on only two stable desk legs.

I sighed and tossed on the green bomber jacket that had been a gift from my mother. She had given it to me when I was in high school, but by some miracle, it still managed to fit. No thanks to my late-night trips to the fridge for extra helpings of chocolate pudding when stressed about money. Lately, the trips to the fridge felt routine.

The carpark shook as I eased out of the driveway with our 2004 paint-chipped blue Ford F-250 truck. I blur of hues of greens and oranges. Fall had claimed most of the leaves, but there were still a few stubborn souls that refused to leave the branches before winter.

On the drive, my mind explored every possible angle on how the motel could stay afloat until December. Eventually, I just sighed. Without any real money, financial ruin was just about six months away at the longest. If nothing changed, then this would be our last Christmas at the motel.

"Thank you, Letty."

I sighed and searched through my wallet. Eventually, I plucked out my sixth from the bottom credit card and willed my eyes not to twitch as I looked at the final amount. The obscenely displayed green numbers on the cash register would haunt me even in my nightmares.

Did I have any credit left on this card? Better question, which card was I sure had any room for such an impressive three-digit number? Lord knows the company card had maxed out three months ago after a milk purchase. I was barely keeping up with the minimum payments on the credit cards. It was a fact that drove the accountant part of me crazy. I subtly crossed my fingers as I begrudgingly handed the credit card over to Letty. Her fingers swiftly swiped the card as I held my breath in anticipation. The little screen blinked in approval and I released a weary sigh.

Letty smiled and asked, "Long week and it's only a Monday?" She knew my mom like an older sister. I had never seen Letty cry in person until my mom's heart to make her worry although the town gossip about the impending foreclosure of the motel had probably already cycled around our small town at least twice.

Instead, I met her kind, faded gaze and replied, "Mondays just aren't for me. I have to figure out what day of the week I like better. How is Frank?"

Letty giggled with near girlish glee and easily accepted the change in subject. Her new miniature poodle had grown in status from Letty's first pet to that of a beloved child.

"Frank is just lovely. He's already mastered shaking hands and is on his way to sit and stay."

"That's very impressive." My heart wasn't really in the conversation, but I tried to return a little of Letty's enthusiasm. For good measure, I added, "I'll see you next week, Letty. Maybe Frank will be an old pro at commands by then."

The crow's feet around Letty's eyes grew more pronounced as she chuckled and waved me out of the store.

My chest felt tight as I reached the truck and mechanically loaded the items into the bed. My arms felt

Unfortunately, my brain felt on the verge of panic, to the point that even driving home felt like a chore. The worn leather of the steering wheel pressed into my face as I sighed in resignation. I was past the point of screaming and hitting the interior of the car. That phase had come and gone months ago after the first credit card declined.

My mother and father had built their dream company and had kept it running smoothly for decades. Now, under my watch, it was crumbling to pieces faster than I could glue them back together. The worst feeling was that it was all my fault. Everyone looked to me for direction and every step I took seemed to drive us further into debt.

Debt was no longer an inanimate concept, but an insatiable monster. It sank its claws into my wallet and devoured the peace within my mind. I no longer panicked as I sat in its jaws and waited to be swallowed whole. On the tip of its tongue waiting for that final mouthful, I was in the eye of the proverbial storm. Hidden and yet naked to the monster all at once. It was only a matter of time.

The outdated television screen cast a faint grey-tinted glow around the room. Chocolate chip ice cream kept finding its way into my mouth as I remained completely transfixed by the screen.

The screen was mostly black as the thin outline of people crept around a supposedly haunted house. Two men tentatively inched from room to room and called out to an otherworldly being. I sighed and decided that it was easier to open a bottle of wine than to change the channel. The remote had managed to disappear for the third time this month.

Three glasses later and the show had me hooked. A woman wrapped in bright purple fabric waved her arms in the middle of a living room and claimed that the spirits within the house spoke to her. She said she had a strong connection to the world beyond. The men from earlier in the television show listened to the ancient woman with undivided attention. The white-haired woman's every word seemed to them like the words from their most beloved family member.

intriguing, the spirit she was talking to claimed to be the original owner of the elaborate house. I tilted my head to the side and tried to recognize why the old place looked so familiar.

A startled gasp escaped my lips as a chair within one of the multiple rooms shown on the show zoomed to the other side. The object clearly moved without the slightest help from human hands. The odd trio on the screen looked as shocked as I felt. My hands found the near empty bottle and diligently added the few droplets to my glass.

Two hours later and the paranormal television show had me absolutely fascinated. I couldn't get enough as I crawled to the edge of the bed and impatiently waited for the next episode.

Luckily, the channel had a marathon of the program dedicated to the premiere of the second season that was set to air the following evening. The visual quality of each show seemed to lessen with each episode, but I was too invested to care about such details. I slumped down to the side of the bed.

from earlier came up to one of the cameras and declared, "This home is most definitely haunted. It should only be visited by the bold and foolhardy."

This was it.

Several unintelligible grumbles later, I stumbled into a standing position which didn't last very long as I tripped on the bed sheets that mercilessly wrapped around my sock-clad ankle.

I whirled around and shushed the sheet for making so much noise, but it was too late.

"Lacy, are you okay?" Stacy's bleary voice called from down the hall. We didn't allow any customers on the top floor so she knew it had to be me. Well, technically we didn't have any people on the levels below, either.

"I'm good." I turned my hazy glare to the troublesome sheets and freed myself from their claw-like grip.

The light whirl of my laptop welcomed my impatient fingers. I waited, filled with eager impish glee. My fingers tapped against its side as it booted up as though the action would help expedite the process. I idea.

An empty bottle of wine fell onto its side as it precariously balanced on the edge of the nightstand. My hands haphazardly slammed against the blaring battery-operated alarm. A pained groan left my lips and rattled my teeth as I sat up and joined the land of the living. A train had hit me. Somehow a train had miraculously built train tracks into my bed during the middle of the night and hit me. It was the only thing that could possibly explain the ringing in my head.

However, judging by the relative organization level of the room and the fact that I was still alive—that option was extremely unlikely.

The wine bottle-turned-culprit swiftly tumbled into the trash can and joined the sticky remains of an ice cream carton. I padded into the bathroom and flicked on the light switch. Even with mental preparation, I still groaned once the fluorescent beams illuminated the sickly sweet pink tiles and reflected the cheery brightness back into my eyes. Light drilled into the back of my skull.

There was only so much duct tape available before pipes needed to be permanently replaced and that ratio had been surpassed months ago. At this point, the pipes were running by sheer willpower and prayer. I rummaged around the medicine cabinet and plucked out two Tylenols as I turned on the shower. The warmth seeped into my bones and lessened the tension within my back. I popped two pills and opened my mouth to swallow some of the scorching stream of water. No need to risk angering the pipe gods by using the sink.

Droplets pooled around my feet as I rinsed off and breathed in a relieved sigh. The dancing in my head had lessened to a low thrum. It made it easier for me to put on some worn out jeans and a lightly ripped turtleneck. Today was drain cleaning day so I wanted to look presentable for my date with a YouTube tutorial video and a 12-foot ladder.

A small question pressed into my consciousness as I tried to remember what had happened the night before. Although at the end of my rope, I was glad to know the motel hadn't been burned down for the insurance money in my wine craze. Stacy had an odd

"Maybe we will get the insurance money on the next bottle of red." I chuckled at my own joke and waved at Jeff as he cut through the fresh vegetables and prepared breakfast for the only guest in attendance.

I shrugged on a threadbare hoodie and walked outside. The shed held several odds and ends that looked frozen in time from another century. But to be fair, the building had been a Victorian era mansion erected during the infamous California Gold rush. The walls had watched over my family and several others before them.

Farming tools from the past scattered around the edges of a slanted workbench like discarded toys. I hoisted the ladder out of the shed and headed in the direction of the motel.

The curved roof came into view as I carefully walked up the icy stone path. Its shingles were missing in several places, but the structure remained regal if not still imposing. The bones of the building had lasted multiple centuries and still had the potential to span at least another 100 years if properly cared for. My eyes lovingly gazed over the once white paint that had slowly turned to a dull grey after years of neglect.

Sparse white hair poked out of the sides of the older man's baseball cap as he pulled out his worn wallet and paid for a room. He smiled at me and then slightly tipped his hat as he hoisted a small duffel bag away from the dated carpeted floor.

He chuckled, "I know it's childish, but I just can't get enough of these attractions. My wife thinks it's a weird obsession, but she's kind enough to let me explore when I get the itch."

I returned a tight smile, "Next time bring your wife. We have great package deals for couples."

With a subtle wave the man headed upstairs and disappeared from sight. He looked harmless enough. Even if his idea of fun was taking a weekend break in a rundown motel without his wife. For all I cared, he could visit as much as he wanted.

I tried to remain calm as the first customer of the week left in search of his room. It was a tad unbelievable, but the meager $78.89 prepaid for two nights gave me hope. My chest felt lighter, and just for a

Stacy walked over to the front desk as her hair stuck to her face. Her drenched black shirt held firm to her body as though the top had been superglued. She looked like a drowned alley cat. Her bottom lip quivered as she opened her palm.

A tiny faucet from the downstairs bathroom had rusted off and broken away from the sink. Apparently at the highest pressure setting, if Stacy's appearance was any indication.

She gently placed the broken faucet on the wooden table and mumbled, "I turned off the water and put a sign on the door that says the bathroom is being cleaned."

I sighed. So much for a little bit of hope. My fingers instinctively itched for my well-used tools as I comforted her, "Don't worry. I'll fix it right now. Can you woman the front desk once you're dry?"

The small joke managed to crack Stacy's pensive mood. "Yeah, that works. I'll be back in a second."

She trotted up the stairs with a little more pep in her step as I worried my bottom lip over my teeth. Today

Three full motel rooms. Three booked rooms. Not one. Not two. Three. I rubbed my chest and counted the number of booked rooms for the ninth time. I wasn't sure if my math skills had suddenly deteriorated or if we were finally having a stroke of luck.

Three full rooms was more occupancy than we had in the entire month of October! I saved the excel sheet and watched as the old computer whirred and the cursor circled in protest. Technology from the dawn of a new millennium had a few setbacks, but the minor inconveniences weren't enough to dampen my joyful mood.

Eventually, the little cursor stopped its tantrum and closed the document. Relieved, I turned my attention to a new task. I checked the list of chores and realized I needed to order a new faucet for the downstairs bathroom. It had lost to the aging power of time just like so many other items in the motel. It was too far gone for duct tape.

"Third time's the charm," I whispered to the empty room and swiftly added the item to the online needed a new faucet judging by the low amount of available online stock. If this didn't work, I'd have to make the shlep over the hill and drive two hours to the next largest town with a general repair store.

"Lacy? The family in room two that just checked in said something about our online website and the history of the hotel. Do you know what they're talking about?" Stacy whisper-yelled as she wiped her hands across the thighs of her skinny jeans and trampled down the staircase with all of the grace of a herd of gazelles.

I didn't. My fingers typed in the name of our hotel into the old computer. Stacy walked around the makeshift desk and peered over my shoulder. We waited for the information to finally load as Stacy tapped her fingers against her hip.

She mumbled, "Forget this." Stacy plucked a piece of grass off of the shoulder of my shirt and sighed.

After what felt like ages, an image of the motel appeared on the dimly lit screen. Stacy grunted in surprise and I wobbled out of the tall wooden bench and

Stacy read, "The Mistletoe Motel dates back almost 200 years and has lived through more than one ghoulish death. Enter if you dare as it even gives the current owners nightmares."

"What did I do?" My voice came out borderline panicked. The room swam as tension and nausea flooded into my body. How could I be so stupid?

I stuttered out, "That was me. I don't really remember, but I know it was me. I had a little bit too much wine and true crime a few weeks ago. I completely forgot I wrote this. I am so sorry, Stacy!"

Not only did the drunk me decide the hotel was haunted, but my inner lush had also declared on the immortal memory of the internet that my father had died in the motel. It wasn't a lie, but that didn't lessen the pain in my chest. Shame filled my body and I couldn't even bring myself to look at Stacy. I didn't want to know what she was thinking.

Stacy leaned into my field of vision and scrolled around the screen. She stopped at a particularly large chunk of text and read it for a few minutes.

hole that was created by my own stupidity.

The silence was killing me, but I didn't dare ruin her concentration. A strand of hair fell out of her bun and covered part of her face like a curtain blowing in the wind.

Eventually, Stacy looked up at me, but her expression remained impassive. Her usually relaxed features concealed a hidden tension that my mind could only twist into a million different meanings. Stacy spoke before I could ask her to put me out of my misery.

Her voice sounded pinched at first and then swelled with confidence, "Well, it's not exactly a lie. Dad did pass away here and I like to think that he is still looking after us. Who is to say that in over 200 years, he's the only person still hanging out around the fireplace when we're all in bed? Energy is never created or destroyed, Lacy. We just become something else."

My frown lines deepened until my two eyebrows nearly pulled together in confusion. A deep hum escaped the back of my throat as I stalled for words, "Let me understand. So you aren't mad that I posted a description

33

Stacy shrugged her shoulders and more strands of hair fell from her loose hairstyle. Pretty soon all of her fair locks would be down and free from her thinly worn hair tie. It felt like a metaphor for how we were holding the motel together; very poorly and likely at the end.

Eventually, she reached out a hand and held mine in a firm grip. Stacy looked at my face and added, "It's not really a lie. More like an off-color truth. Besides, we haven't had this many guests in years and they're all coming in hopes of seeing something slightly supernatural. It's not like we can guarantee that even if were actually haunted. Ghosts can't show up on command. Besides, the guests are not actually expecting anyone to walk through the walls or for their beds to levitate in the middle of the night. That package would cost extra."

A small smile curved my lips upward and away from their typically downward position. I hugged Stacy and quickly rubbed a few traitorous tears away as they threatened to turn from a trickle into a steady stream.

were both Pondwaters, after all.

Heavy footsteps clamored against the old wood and Jeffrey leisurely ambled into the room. He was covered in a thin layer of sweat. He was obviously preparing dinner and it was one of the very first meal services the motel had witnessed in years. Jeffrey blotted away the perspiration on his neck and playfully wiggled his eyebrows.

Stacy squirmed around in my arms once she noticed his goofy reaction and groaned, "You gorgeous idiot. Can't you see I am having a sisterly moment with Lacy?"

He puffed out his chest and placed his strong arms near his waist in a superhero pose. Jeffrey teased, "Can I join?"

I laughed, "Maybe next time."

Days moved in a blur as I puttered along with repairs and guided curious guests to the rooms. I stood outside and wrestled with the rose bushes. Most of the guests were still inside for the early portion of the morning and the ebb of eager patrons gave me the infrequent opportunity to fix up the garden.

I gripped the rose cutters closer to the base of the plant and tried to properly prune it. Momentarily surprised, I hissed in pain. A small thorn pricked the sensitive skin underneath my nail and pain shot through my finger. It reverberated up my arm until the pain reached deep into my shoulder like a persistent heartbeat. I sighed. This wasn't my first work related accident.

"Do you need a hand?"

A tall, blonde stranger stood near the stone pathway that led to the motel. He casually stuffed his hands deep into his dark blue jean pockets.

I momentarily stood with my pricked hand stuck in the air as if I had accidentally stumbled into the middle of a robbery.

Stunned, I held the rose bush cutters high in the air and narrowed my eyes. Something about the stranger felt familiar, but I couldn't put my finger on why. After a few seconds of contemplation, I figured that I would definitely remember someone so handsome. He had to be new.

"I'll consider that to mean maybe later." He brushed his blonde locks as a cold gust of wind rattled past the wind chimes and flew directly into the newcomer's face.

I coughed, "Yeah, some help would be great. Thanks."

The man, about two or three years older than me, walked over, mindful of keeping to the motel's stone path. I observed the last detail with slight satisfaction.

I handed the rose cutters to the stranger and added, "I should tell you, I don't usually give such sharp objects to strangers. We are in the middle of nowhere and everything."

A deep chuckle passed the handsome stranger's smirking mouth. The sight momentarily left me giddy. What was wrong with me?

needed to be pruned. He leaned down and easily set about the task.

In seconds, he had finished the entire row of rose bushes. He wiped a small bead of sweat from his strong brow and handed the cutters back. "Hi, I'm Evan. I own the garage in town. I wanted to see what all of the commotion was about."

He held out a roughened hand for me to shake. I momentarily stood with the clippers pointed up into the air. To any passersby, it would look like I was seconds away from chopping off Evan's hand. Luckily, there were no passersby and I was in a relatively good mood.

"Thank you."

I placed the cutters by my ransacked toolbox and reached out to shake Evan's hand. His palm easily engulfed my smaller digits about two times over. I hadn't considered my hands petite or clean, but compared to Evan's calloused and grease-blackened hands, mine looked ready for the MET Gala.

"Hi, Evan. It's nice to meet you. What do you mean by 'commotion'? We do have more customers than usual, but it's nothing too rowdy."

Is it true that this place is haunted? It's the talk of the town down at Betty's Diner."

At the mention of the diner, I wiped my suddenly sweaty palms on my jeans. "Wow, I always forget how quickly news travels around this tiny place."

"Well, it's not hard to become the top news story when there is no news to begin with."

Suddenly, ice cold water attacked us from every direction. I screeched in surprise and stood up in the middle of the rose bush planter. The sprinklers had turned on two hours too early and I scrambled to move the tools out of the way.

Evan quickly followed my lead and trampled up the wooden porch steps with the rose cutters and ladder in tow. He hefted the ladder onto his shoulder and then quickly propped it near the other corner of the motel so that it would be out of sight from motel guests.

Evan's white shirt and dark puffer jacket looked soaked and his once surfer chic hair now made him look more like a nearly-drowned Pomeranian. Judging by his clothes, I was sure that I looked just as bad and burst out laughing. My stomach ached as another wave of laughter directly on the crotch of my jeans. Just lovely.

I wiped a small tear from the corner of my eye and vaguely pointed at the wooden ladder, "You know that the ladder can get wet, right?"

A blush crept up the back of Evan's neck as he sheepishly admitted, "I panicked."

"Thank you, Evan. That's the most thoughtful version of panic I have seen. Here, please come inside at least for a cup of coffee. You'll freeze to death and that can't happen. We already have too many ghosts around this place." I sent him a playful wink and held the door open.

For once, I decided the motel could survive without my anxiety-induced cosmetic repairs. At least for a few minutes. Something about Evan just felt too interesting to dismiss. Maybe it was just the fact that he was the first man I had seen who was even remotely close to my age. Maybe I found him interesting because he wasn't focused on my now soaked bottom as I walked around the motel.

Jeffrey was the only man even near his 20s who spent more than four seconds at the motel, but he didn't younger, built-in brother.

I allowed that train of thought to drop as we entered the foyer. Exhausted, I sighed in relief as the warmth of the motel helped thaw my frozen fingers. I rubbed my arms together and then fully looked at Evan.

Apparently, he had taken the brunt of the sprinklers and looked closer to a drowned cat than a handsome thirty-something adult. Droplets of water puddled around his feet.

I walked further into the living room and laughed. My gaze wandered, looking from the drenched crotch of my own pants back to Evan's ruined clothes and I burst into another round of laughter. Evan joined in and teased, "I didn't know you scared so easily."

"I'm only scared of people who don't know that wooden ladders are allowed to get wet."

Stacy peaked into the room and blanched at the sight. Small rivulets of water wrapped around the room from the front door and led all the way into the living room. A playful smile crept onto her face as she sent me a cheeky wink.

emphatic wave.

To save face, I quickly coaxed, "Hey, Stacy. Come meet Evan. He owns the garage in town and was just helping me with the rose bushes. Apparently, the automatic sprinklers are off by more than an hour."

Stacy waltzed into the room and her dry, healthy hair cheerfully bounced behind her. "Hi! It's so nice to meet you. You look really familiar."

Evan shook her hand. "I was born and raised here, but I left for college. We probably saw each other around town as kids. Time sure flies."

Stacy laughed as she took a step back. "Everything changes, but at the same time everything stays the same."

Evan laughed as he playfully nudged my shoulder. "I guess that's the beauty of a small town. Besides the fact that even the slightest bit of gossip travels faster than a brush fire during fire season."

I groaned, "You can say that again. At least we don't have to worry about catching fire anytime soon."

with the palm of my hand as I watched Evan shiver.

"Stay right here. You can borrow some spare clothes so you don't catch a cold. It's the least I can do."

I was about to leave the room when Stacy intervened, "Don't worry! I can bring both of you spare clothes. Stay down here. You'll just track water all over the place."

She scuttled out of the room and I arched an eyebrow in amazement. Since when did Stacy ever jump into action to prevent something as menial as a wet floor?

Skeptical, I narrowed my eyes at my sister's poorly hidden matchmaking attempt, but I didn't bother saying anything. For once, I didn't disagree with Stacy.

"Your sister seems nice." Evan shrugged his shoulders as he glanced outside the living room window.

The shed in the back corner of the field was just barely visible behind a random pile of snow. Each winter, the shed seemed to disappear from the massive yard as several feet of snow covered the little wooden structure. Usually, only the tin roof was visible by

Today, the outside just looked like a frigid yard with an extremely dilapidated shed. I walked over to Evan and stared out the window.

I sighed, "Stacy is the peanut butter to my jelly and also the oil to my water. We don't always see everything the same way, but she always has my back. She really handled the passing of our father better than I did."

Evan's blue gaze turned to me as a deep sadness crossed his gaze. He nodded, "I am sure your father was an amazing man. It's a small town, so people talk. He had a funeral fit for a king."

A slow smile crept along the edges of my lips, but didn't fully reach my eyes. My father had had a truly heartwarming ceremony. People even three towns over had traveled the distance to pay their respects. He was just so kind that everyone wanted to be in his presence. He had been the sun to two young and gangly daughters.

I playfully shoved Evan's shoulder. "That does make me the princess of this castle along with Stacy."

I dramatically waved in the direction of the rest of the house and declared, "A glorious kingdom with

A small tear threatened to fall so I slightly tilted my head to the side so Evan couldn't see my odd moment of vulnerability. Unfortunately, it wasn't that easy.

Evan rubbed the back of his neck and averted his eyes back to the window. He gave me a moment to collect my composure as he spoke, "I could help with the sinks. I really know a few things about pipes and would be happy to fix yours for a cup of coffee and dry clothes."

"Oh, so now you're offering to fix her pipes? This conversation moved along fast." Stacy's mischievous face popped into the room. Her bright eyes held laughter as she held out some of Jeffrey's warmer clothes to Evan. The sweatpants and white long sleeve shirt looked extremely large. Surprisingly, the items appeared to fit when Evan held the items up against his body for a visual check.

Stacy nodded her head in approval and added, "Don't worry. We will even give you dry clothes that fit if you need to size up or down."

45

familiar to me, but I was too cold to care.

"I'll be right back. Evan, you can use the downstairs bathroom." I hustled out of the room and locked myself in the broom cabinet next to the spiral staircase. I didn't want to put water all over the carpet. Instead, I pulled on the long string and harsh light poured into the cramped space from a singular bulb.

"Keep it together, Lace. He's sweet, but you hardly know him. He could still be a random murderer or an undercover motel reviewer."

The words felt ridiculous as soon as I said them out loud. In my gut, I felt that Evan was a good person. I just hoped I wouldn't live to regret trusting that hunch.

My fingers pried open the closet door as I blindly bumped into a burly back. I apologized, "Sorry. I just came out of the closet."

Jeffrey frowned in slight confusion and noted, "Good to know."

He ambled into the living room with a tray of coffee and hot chocolate in tow. Oh, no. Stacy was going to make this a thing.

I impatiently tugged on the new dry pants and looked in the hallway mirror. My palms felt sweaty so I brushed them down the sides of my now water-free jeans and muttered, "What am I doing?"

Voices from the other room quickly ruined my apprehension. There was no point in hiding in the hallway.

"I'll have hot chocolate. Thanks. I didn't get your name. I'm Evan."

Jeffrey shrugged his shoulders, "I'm Jeffrey. Resident cook and full-time Victorian motel repairman."

hallway.

"Very funny, Jeff. We all know that Lacy has you beat in that department. If she's not trying to raise money for the roof then she's fixing my mistakes and replacing meat that I spoiled by leaving the locker door wide open."

I turned the corner and watched as Stacy winced at the memory. I instantly cringed at her discomfort and felt bad for being so rough on her earlier in the week. It really was an honest mistake. Expensive, but still an honest mistake.

"What did I miss?" I entered the living room and sat down on the sofa. The comfortable seat molded against my sore body and my back sunk further into the cushions.

Evan sat down on the opposite side of the sofa and gently blew across the hot coco as steam emerged from the cup.

Jeffrey casually wrapped an arm around Stacy's middle as he took a leisurely sip of coffee. The faint remnants of coffee, at least. The nearly white liquid

A small smile crossed my lips. Jeffrey was definitely a softie and Stacy had found someone perfectly compatible with her. The duo was practically inseparable.

"So how long have of you worked here?" Evan forced out the question with something close to feigned curiosity.

Stacy sipped her black coffee as she appeared to mull over the question. "We really started when our dad grew ill. After he passed, we didn't really think about it. We just fell into working at the motel."

"A heck of a thing to fall into."

"Yeah, but there are worse jobs. This motel has a ton of potential. We just need a fair chance and a little more in the bank. Of course, isn't that what most small business owners say?" Stacy chuckled as she nudged her mug in Evan's direction. The action looked similar to an air cheers.

He laughed, "Yeah, owning a business definitely requires some thick skin. The first two years with the garage, I felt like I was walking around in the dark.

Stacy smiled, "So you came full-circle."

"What do you mean?"

"You started out in the dark without a clue and now you know the business so well that the dark doesn't bother you."

Evan laughed, "I never looked at it that way. Maybe we don't need to fear the dark once we finally know what it holds."

The scent of ancient books and aged wood drifted through the poorly ventilated air. For a library just over a century old, it wasn't that bad. I couldn't remember the last time that I had stepped through these creaky double doors, but countless memories flooded around the back of my mind. They all melded together and I desperately tried to shut them out. I hated remembering the past, so I tried to stomp down old memories as quickly as possible. Especially, now that they all tended to blend together over the years.

In my memories, a tiny Lacy poured over the historical section and diligently tried to decide which ten books to rent at a time. Tiny fingers gripped around leather binding for hours at a time until the old librarian, Mrs. Smith, shooed me out for the evening. The smallest hint of a smile threatened to creep along my lips at the faint reminiscences of a simpler time.

Luckily, a thoughtful middle-aged woman accidentally ruined that potentially painful path. She lowered her reading glasses and smiled. Her lipstick

"Hello, dear. Can I help you with anything?" She gave a small polite wave that inspired my feet to move closer to the checkout desk.

I shoved my hands deep into the pockets of my jacket. Fingers numbly fished around for a few seconds as my brain struggled to reel in my thoughts. On the line, I replied, "Hi, I'm looking for old news stories about the town."

The older woman looked away deep in thought. She pursed her lips and the action deepened the fine lines into valleys on her painted mouth. Eventually, she turned back around and directed, "Look in the newspaper archives. Here, come with me. They should be near the back."

With a simple crook of her finger, the older woman named Maggie hustled out from behind the counter and walked with purpose to the farthest back corner. At least, her name tag read as Maggie. Her gait made me question her age as she spryly maneuvered around piles of new books and hunkered down customers.

and poorly illuminated the area. Stacks upon stacks of papers and old newspaper sections remained precariously elevated from the floor by barely held together shelves.

With a flourish of slim fingers, Maggie turned around and smiled, "Here you are. Just let me know if you need any help or would like me to print something for you."

"Thank you. I will."

Overwhelmed, I took off my jacket and placed it on the back of the sturdy wooden chair. I didn't really know where to start, but the library felt like the right place to begin.

I mumbled just under my breath, "Too far invested to escape now. Time to learn the history of our old motel. It's like a billion years old. There has to be at least one possibly interesting ghost story around."

It wasn't really a lie. But what had been placed online after too much wine and true crime was also definitely not the truth. These wrinkly papers hopefully had the power to turn that little fib around.

years, but the four decades of history seemed like child's play in the grand scheme of things. The motel had first been created in the 1860s and now spanned well over a century and a few decades..

Were newspapers even legible after a century? Did the paper crumble up and disintegrate? Was it possible that the ink eventually turned invisible with time?

Questions swirled around in my mind as I tentatively looked around. I felt as if the file cabinets had exploded into the air within my very own mental version of a library. Papers whirled and spun down to the ground in a flurry of papery chaos. There was no order. It was simply complete chaos at its finest.

Images of Ford Thunderbirds and Chevrolet Bel Airs parked proudly on the main street of town and greeted my field of vision. They were frozen in time and silently stood watch like large watchful sentinels. The 1950s were a lifetime ago, but it still wasn't nearly far enough back to get a full history of the motel. I was still missing about 100 years of history.

born. My parents had been the children of World War II fighters and diligent factory workers. It was a combination that had somehow created my artsy and frugal parents. Some would say that they had been conventionally scrappy, but I preferred the term frugal. Well, except when it came to Stacy and me. Mom had always caved, spoiling us with whatever we needed from backpacks to tasty late night snacks.

My fingers delved through the newspapers as if on autopilot until they finally found the page that I had been so eagerly searching for. A small byline less than three sentences long read:

Luna Smith, born on April 12 1951 to Harold and Hannah Jones. Luna is their first child and will be baptized in the church this coming Sunday.

A fleck of moisture threatened to escape my eyes as I looked down in a strange combination of awe and shock. It was difficult to imagine my mother as a baby or even something other than a fully-formed adult with likes and preferences and a very strong eye for financial discrepancies in the motel books. The one thing

Mom had left the town for a school only a few hours away and had returned a handful of years later with my father in tow. They had met by some sheer freak accident. It wasn't a world-stopping event or anything memorably chaotic, but in some tiny way their fate meeting had changed history. My mother had bumped into my father at a café. It had been the day of her mathematics test on a day that she usually never bothered to stop for an afternoon snack. My father had stopped into the cafe because his tire had lost its air a few miles back and he needed to call for help. The rest was history. It was no wonder that they had loved our own small diner so much. It had surely reminded them of the day that they had first met.

My fingers twitched over the paper and traced each letter of my mom's name with a sense of reverence. Eventually, I walked over to my purse and took a photo of the announcement with my camera. It was definitely going to be framed back at the motel.

The task was another item added to the already nearly never-ending to-do list. At least, this task didn't involve leaky pipes or peeling paint from the outside of announcement.

I mumbled, "Priorities. Find the oldest newspapers, Lacy. You were a star accountant, finding missing numbers and digging through details are two of your specialties."

The brief personal pep talk seemed to soothe my fingers enough so that they picked up speed across every page and paper spine. The longer that I looked through the enormous stack, the more brittle the pages became. Two copies of each and every town newspaper since what seemed like the birth of our little land in the sticks, remained placed away from sight and out of view from the collective memory of the town. The news slowly grew too old as the townspeople grew too young to recall such events.

Slowly, the car models grew less recognizable and the picture quality turned grainy. It was a subtle shift, but still noticeable enough when placed in comparison to the most most recent newspaper covers. Eventually, even the images on the front cover stories were replaced with massive headlines in bold black font and lengthy bylines that seemed to tease and tantalize the

I glanced at the dated top right corner and sighed. It was still only a newspaper article from the 1940s.

I glanced down as the digits on my phone screen. The screen illuminated a time slightly different than I had expected. Several hours had gone by in a blur of poorly guided exploration. Most of the newspapers were in chronological order, but there were a few that had managed to meander out of place. Close, but not completely perfect.

The stacks grew less and less impressive and the paper felt more brittle. Eventually, the newspapers were even protected within plastic folders. I stared at the last newspaper. This didn't make any sense. Shock riled the back of my mind into an irritated frenzy. What happened here?

The paper trail abruptly ended in the middle of 1932 without any further explanation. There wasn't the slightest hint to what had possibly happened to the rest of the newspapers. Curious, I stretched out my sore limbs and picked up my belongings.

After several hours, the scent of old paper and aging wood was barely perceptible to my senses. It whirled around my nose like an outdated reminder or a mysteriously misplaced and barely missed sticky note.

Stacks of books appeared nearly untouched as I slowly crept out of the least used area of the library. It was as if someone had roped off the entire back of the library with yellow crime scene tape and instructed every patron to remain on the other side. The history of this sleepy town felt oddly off limits. Access to the information almost felt discouraged even though that wasn't the truth seeing as Mrs. Smith had been more than accommodating.

Once at the front desk, I scraped together my best friendly smile. "Hi, Maggie. Do you know what

Maggie turned in my direction as a small frown furrowed her thin brows as she muttered, "Oh, dear. I believe that the fire most likely ruined the rest of the archives."

"The fire?" I couldn't remember a large fire that had ever threatened the cabin-like library. It stood in the center of town like a proud beacon that illuminated the darkness with its beams of wisdom that reached almost every corner until the very town limits. At least, that's how I viewed one of my most cherished childhood haunts.

Pun intended.

Maggie added, "Yes, there had been a dreadful fire during the early 1960s. It had threatened to ruin the rest of the town. The quick flames had nearly pummeled the building into the ground. Luckily, there had been a joint fire brigade exercise with the neighboring town just down the street. Thanks to sheer luck, the fire had been extinguished in minutes. Unfortunately, some of the older material had already been lost."

Kind old eyes stared at something in the distance. It was a memory that I could not follow so I shoulders and made her look somehow smaller than how I had perceived her at the start of the day.

Suddenly, she exclaimed, "Oh! I remember! How about we go down into the basement and search the deep archives? It's possible that there are a few newspapers down there. That's where the oldest documents are hidden from the casual reader. You wouldn't believe how many kids like to doodle in the margins of these books when they get bored."

An excited smile electrified the corners of my lips, "I can imagine. That's perfect, Maggie." The purse that slumped down my shoulder at an awkward angle no longer felt like a nuisance as I hefted the straps higher than where they had started and waited for Maggie to lead the way.

She gave a small patient chuckle and explained, "I can show you when it's time to close. There are several people today and I don't want to miss them if they need to check out a new book."

Only partially deflated, I nodded my head and prepared to head back to the rickety wooden table in the back corner.

chorus before my mortified fingers finally managed to grip the phone.

Maggie held a less than bemused smile as she looked on from behind the front desk. She nodded her head in dismissal as I waved to her in a befuddled combination of both an apology and goodbye. I headed out the wooden door and clicked accept.

Afternoon sunlight danced around the park playground across the street. It spun and reflected from the shiny new swing set and silver colored circular slide. Children giggled in the distance with glee as they joyfully ran around the newly refurbished park. The calm of the outdoors managed to settle my frazzled nerves. I had completely forgotten about lowering the volume on my phone before entering the library.

"Hello?"

"Can you hear me?" Jeffrey's tension-filled voice called from the other end of the phone. He sounded stressed as if he was curling the phone tighter between his large palm with every passing moment.

sister's phone number. "What's wrong, Jeffrey?"

A brief pause. Eventually, he answered, "Stacy, fell off the roof."

"What do you mean that the ladder mysteriously moved?" This didn't make any sense in terms of falling off a roof. That was a ridiculous explanation. I absently wondered if the ladder had skid against the drainage pipes. I knew that they tended to get slippery this time of year.

Stacy threw her arms up into the air in frustration as her ankle remained propped up on a mountain of poorly arranged pillows. She lounged on the sofa like a regal courtier as several people, including me, congregated around her in the living room. From ice cream to ice packs, no request was too small.

She turned her tired blue eyes back in my direction as her ponytail tilted off to one side as she explained, "I told you. It was almost like it had a mind of its own! I was just about to climb down, but the ladder collapsed to the ground just as I was stepping over to use it. There is something very strange going on here. I think this place really might be haunted, Lacy."

I took a moment to understand what Stacy wanted to tell me and blanked. Impossible. Even my overcommitted with a wine bottle.

"Are you sure that it wasn't one of those twins in room number three? I am pretty sure that they plucked a few of the front desk pens from the holder and used them as darts. It's possible that those two little demons did it. They're like a twisted version of *The Parent Trap*."

Stacy rolled her eyes as Jeffrey entered the room and placed a new ice pack on her inflamed ankle. The swollen area was so inflamed that it looked like a miniature Thanksgiving Day Parade float compared to the rest of her other uninjured appendage.

Cringe.

"Thanks, Jeffrey."

He simply nodded and settled back down into the flowery upholstered chair that remained closest to the sofa. He gingerly reached out and squeezed her hand.

"You know that your sister is right, Lacy. There is something weird happening at this motel. I can't explain it, but it's just not the same." Jeffrey looked at me with large pleading brown eyes.

"The energy is different, Lacy. We invited something into the motel with that online impossible.

I quipped, "Oh, no. That is absolutely not what happened. I added a little flair to the motel and attracted two potential demon children to unnecessarily harass us. I don't regret the income, but I'm really starting to regret the little kids."

"It wasn't the twins. You just don't like them because they said that your jeans were out of style."

Maybe there was a little truth to that statement.

Stacy added, "Where were you today?"

I paused, "Out in town. What happened to holding the ladder as you climbed down?"

The slight deflection seemed to work. Stacy's shoulders bunched in irritation as she took the bait. There wasn't much of a point in adding more fuel to the possible paranormal fire. It seemed to be burning on a low simmer in the back of both Stacy's and Jeffrey's minds.

Incredible. Now there were two people in desperate need of a loony bin or therapy and I couldn't even afford new paint for the motel, let alone two

Stacy shook her head and her blonde locks moved in every direction like a waterfall. She added, "Let me explain. You probably haven't noticed it because you are just so into rescuing the motel that anything else falls to the side of the tracks. I bet that you didn't even realize that Evan was flirting with you." She gave me the most haughty smug younger sister glance as she arched a singular eyebrow.

"He was just being nice! Evan said that he just wanted to see what all of the fuss was about. Apparently, the entire town is talking about what's happening up here. Now, he'll just think that the motel has questionable sprinklers and an incompetent co-owner that likes to roll around in the rosebushes."

"Fine. You don't need to admit to anything right now, but just keep an open mind. He really is handsome. Right, Jeffrey?"

"Sure."

Stacy rolled her eyes and then locked them on Jeffrey with an expression that read something along the lines of help me out. Undeterred, Stacy fixes her stern

"I can't just prove that someone was being nice to me. Just take my word for it. Also, we need to take inventory later this week."

"Lacy, you are changing the subject and it shows."

"Fine, how about I'll ask Evan to grab a bite to eat if we ever run into each other in town? Satisfied, Ms. Bossy?"

"Deal." Lacy leaned up from her position on the sofa and stuck out her pinky finger. I extended my own and we locked digits in the most official way to solidify a sisterly agreement. A pinky promise.

Hopefully, I won't see Evan until after Christmas. There was too much work at the motel to make time for a potential holiday romance.

Fluorescent lights flickered as I loaded a few unappetizing frozen meals into my cart. It seemed like the easy fix to handling long work nights in comparison to the more expensive alternatives such as pizza delivery or takeout. I dispassionately flipped around the packaged frozen pizza and mouthed what was supposed to be the long list of ingredients, but it just sounded like something from a science experiment. Well, it was safe to assume that this pizza would be around much longer than the two bags of spinach at the front of my cart. Much longer.

"This must be what they make Twinkies out of."

"Oh, absolutely. They're probably made by the same parent company. When I don't have time to cook, I usually just buy the Veggiefresh Promise brand. It doesn't keep as long in the freezer, but I can get through the list of ingredients without needing to reference a dictionary."

Oh, no. I knew that smooth casual voice as it traveled the slim length of the aisle. I subconsciously placed a few stray strands of hair behind my ear as if that

"Veggiefresh Promise? I've never heard of that. Did Letty decide to try something new?"

"Yep, I convinced her last month to give it a try. Now, she loves it. Letty says that the they even sell twice as fast compared to the other frozen pizzas. Here."

Evan retracted one of his hands from the small red shopping carts and opened the freezer doors. He rummaged around and retrieved a bright green and red pizza box with swirly writing and a logo that was designed using different vegetables.

"That's a very literal marketing strategy."

Evan simply shrugged his shoulders as he handed me the box and said, "It gets the job done. Trust me."

Suddenly, a brilliant plan popped into the back of my head. It wasn't exactly what Stacy had suggested, but it would still do the trick. I sucked my bottom lip between my teeth in apprehension and exhaled.

"Hey, Evan. What about we make a friendly bet about this pizza?"

"What do you have in mind?"

Evan prodded, "But what if I'm wrong and you don't like the pizza?"

"If you're wrong about the green pizza then you can make it up to me with a soda. It will help balance out all of the green and healthy stuff."

Evan leaned back on the balls of his feet and then hefted his weight back to the front of his shoes as he whistled low in the back of his throat. He added, "You drive a hard bargain, Lacy, but you most definitely have yourself a deal."

He stuck out his hand and for a moment I just stared at him until my brain finally realized that we needed to shake hands in order for it to be a deal. I stuck my hand out and watched as his larger palm easily encircled mine.

"I'll try it out and let you know, Evan. Thanks for the tip. The tasteless microwave food was slowly driving me insane. Not that I'm really sane after trying to keep the motel together when it's probably better just easier to sell it, but still."

Overshare. Total overshare. Why did I just say that? A strange off-brand version of panic, similar to the door of the supermarket and never look back. The somewhat smeared windows of the glass door on Letty's business had never looked so attractive.

Unfortunately, leaving would mean admitting defeat to Stacy. There was no way that I wanted to lose my cool and only further prove to her that I had lost my nerves when it came to dating and dealing with the opposite sex. If it wasn't about account balances or the motel, it seemed that I had lost my touch.

Without missing a beat, Evan pulled me back into the present and asked, "How can I help? I have a few more workers at the shop than usual so I have some time on my hands. Want to go over to the diner and talk about the motel? It sounds like something from the pages of a Victorian romance novel."

"Is that your favorite guilty-pleasure genre of books? Mine is more on the side of supernatural mystery, but romance novels are a close second."

Evan made a surprised guffaw as his blonde eyebrows sharply rose and fell around his amused blue orbs. The action almost made his face appear like one of those cartoon characters that tended to overreact in a straight white teeth. He chuckled, "I can't reveal a guilty pleasure before having a meal with you. It's much too personal."

I shuffled my feet and gripped the handle of the shopping cart as a bitter awareness slunk into my bones. The quaint diner on First Avenue had been my mother's favorite spot in town. In two years, I still had never returned to the red leather booths or played a song on the ancient jukebox that sat in the corner. It tended to get stuck in the middle of songs on particularly warm and sunny days. That would be nice, but it wasn't happening.

The thought of nosey stares from loose acquaintances filled with curiosity and sadness instantly dulled my appetite. It was hard enough to go to the supermarket without running into every single person that had ever come into contact with my parents. There were just too many stories that managed to bring them back to life and then seemed to rip a chunk of the healing wound across my heart wide open all over again. Emotional stitches weren't intended to be plucked and pulled at every opportunity.

much my mother had always loved saving bugs on the playground from pesky little boys with magnifying glasses. A brave gentle soul.

Instead, I preferred to hide in the motel and use it as a makeshift bunker where I had indefinitely decided to hunker down and wait out the commotion. The wait seemed endless and the town incessant.

"Maybe another time, Evan. I need to get back to the motel and make sure everything is in order. Especially now that Stacy injured her ankle."

Thick golden honey colored brows pulled together as an unreadable emotion crossed Evan's features and swiftly morphed into concern at the mention of Stacy's name. "Is your sister okay?"

I waved my hand in a slightly dismissive manner around my face and explained, "She fell from the roof. Stacy claims that it was something strange and supernatural, but I have my money on two rambunctious and horribly oblivious kids that are staying at the motel."

"A mystery at the Mistletoe Motel, that's very fitting."

enough to even make the town papers."

"You never know, stranger things have happened."

"That's true."

"Stay safe, Lacy. I hope that your sister feels better soon."

"Thanks, Evan. I'm sure that she will. She has the endurance and agility of a gazelle."

"What about you?"

The question momentarily caught me off guard as I absently picked at the plastic corner of the bread package in my cart. Eventually, a teasing smile escaped as I replied, "I think that I'm closer to a raccoon. A tad nocturnal with a tendency to eat junk food and very resourceful in most situations."

Evan burst into a deep belly laugh. After a few seconds, he tilted his head to the side as if he were inspecting my features in a different light. For once, I didn't shy away from such an examination since part of me was sure that it was from a flattering perspective. Another part of me just wanted to be seen. Which in

"What about you?"

"What about me?"

"Are you a raccoon or a gazelle?"

"Definitely a raccoon. If not, maybe a Labrador."

"A Labrador makes sense. You definitely have the shiny hair for it."

"Thanks. I hope to see you around town."

"You will, Evan."

For once, it was a promise that I was excited to keep. It wasn't exactly a dinner date with Evan, but it was close. Well, closer than I had been in years and technically he had offered a meal since he had suggested the diner. The frozen solid Veggiefresh Promise pizza seemed nearly gourmet as I glanced at it's green and red packaging and prepared to checkout. The pizza was a start, but of what, I wasn't sure.

"Stacy, where did you put the extra paper? The printer is low and I can't print out this excel sheet."

A petulant cry from the living room told me that Stacy didn't know where she had last placed the stack of new printer paper. Incredible.

"I don't know. Look near the printer."

"Stacy, I already searched the office area twice! You are seriously so unorganized."

"Well, did you ever consider that you're too organized? Maybe it's just hiding from you and your neat freak ways."

A beat of silence later, "You lost five pounds of printer paper! If you weren't stuck on the sofa for the next week, then I'd make you go look for it."

Stacy sarcastically called, "Send out the search party."

Luckily, the guests and Jeffrey had all wandered out into town for the day. The only witness to our little squabble galloped vigilantly above the fireplace. A figurine of an old western woman remained proud. She sat bareback on a wild dark horse as both of their hair on the horse. I had gazed at her for hours as she commanded the attention of the living room from above the fireplace and ruled her kingdom with effortless grace.

Suddenly, a rolled-up sock landed on my shoulder. Stacy sat propped on the pillows as a smug look graced her usually collected features. She arched a blonde eyebrow in an act of mischievous defiance as she declared, "Earth to space cadet. Come back to the planet. You still need to find the printer paper and swing by the kitchen. The ice on my ankle is getting all melty."

I curled up my lower lip like the drawing of a castle bridge. I bit down on a snippy comment as it threatened to burst past the lowered gate of my teeth. Don't do it, be the older sister.

Instead, I plucked the sock from my shoulder and hurled it back in Stacy's direction. Her muffled shriek told me that I had hit my target. The sock connected perfectly with her cherubic and currently insufferable face.

"I'll get you some ice. You big baby."

main desk and picked up the phone. Hopefully, it was another customer that was curious about the buzz surrounding the motel.

"Hello?"

This didn't sound like a typical reservation inquiry. I pressed the receiver closer to my ear and clarified, "I'm sorry. Who is this?"

A somewhat distant voice from the other end called, "Hello! This is the Scare Squad speaking. We heard that your motel is haunted and would love to come visit with our film crew."

Ice rushed deep down into my veins as I struggled to understand if a strange nightmare had finally happened. This had to be a dream. My knuckles turned white as I gripped the receiver tighter and tried to cough out an excuse or explanation, but my mind felt blank and foggy with panic.

"Are you still there? The phone connection is a tad wonky." A slightly southern twang rang out and spurred my limbs into a frenzied flurry of motion.

"Yes, I'm still on the line. How did you find The Mistletoe Motel?"

"Oh, it's on a ghost fanatic website and you will be pleased to know that your motel is currently ranked number two for scare authenticity in the entire United the show. We can sort out the logistics later. Do you have a specific date in mind for us to film the episode?"

I felt like there was a massive police helicopter hovering above my shoulders and I was trapped in the spotlight. It was as if the universe had caught me and placed me underneath the unflinching beam for my crime. I couldn't decide if the universe had truly placed me in the spotlight of a police helicopter or the stage lights of a main circus performance.

It was a dangerous position to dangle so precariously from such a high tightrope, but I didn't dare look down. I opened my mouth and decided to keep walking to the other side. "Yes, I believe that some time before Christmas would be best. That way you can see the holiday decor and it will most likely be snowing by that time of year."

The disjointed peppy voice cooed, "That sounds marvelous. Where can I fax the upcoming information and details?"

My mind functioned on autopilot as I provided the necessary details like Icarus drawn to the light of the sun. Eventually, if I moved too close then I would fall happen. I wouldn't let that happen.

The silent vow strengthened my stubborn fortitude and resolve. If they wanted a haunted motel, then they were most definitely going to receive a haunted motel.

Without thinking, I added, "My sister also runs the motel so let me talk with her and then we can go from there. It was so nice speaking to you." My voice trailed off in uncertainty.

"Magatha. Magatha Everhope, but all of my friends call me Magda. I must say that I am thrilled to be able to see your motel in person. The online reviews most definitely do not disappoint. Missing items and unexplained changes in temperature? Sounds like a classic apparition, but of course our team will be the judge of that."

My voice accidentally trilled up another octave as I added, "Of course."

The line turned into a dial tone as I drew in a ragged breath. My feet turned into jelly as I melted down into the well-worn seat behind the front desk. "What have I done?"

the old wooden floorboards as if the slabs of defeated trees were the most interesting thing on the planet.

A slightly winded voice called from a few paces away, "What happened to the ice?"

"We have bigger problems than the ice, Stacy." I slumped further down into the already indented chair. The back cushion still perfectly conformed to my mother's figure as if it was simply waiting for its true owner to return from a quick trip to the grocery store. In some ways, I suppose that I was also waiting for my mother to return. Few things around the motel had actually evolved or moved into the twenty-first century. Maybe that needed to change.

"Lacy, what's wrong?" Blue concerned eyes entered my field of vision as Stacy struggled to level her gaze with my own.

I rolled my eyes and hopped off the bar-height chair as I nudged her with my shoulder. She gratefully took the offer and snuggled into the recently vacated chair, but her eyes still held a barely contained worry. Stacy reached into one of the pockets of her sweatpants and retrieved an unopened packet of candy. She lifted it higher into the air and offered, "Do you want a jelly bean? They're the good kind and not the store brand."

gesture, but it meant a ton since they were Stacy's favorite comfort snack. As a kid, she had frequently hid them all over her room, in tiny little stashes. A fact that our mother had loved in the summer just as much as the ants that were attracted to the usually sticky and semi-melted globs. Delicious.

"Thanks."

Slow chews. I looked at nothing in particular as my eyes drifted in and out of focus. Eventually, I swallowed after the singular jelly bean was efficiently ground into dust by my back molars.

"You'll never guess who was just on the phone."

"Who? Was it Evan? Did he finally get up the nerve to ask you on a date? That's a little out of the blue, but still exciting. You don't look excited. Why don't you look excited?"

Stacy was right, my face pinched near the corners as if I had just tasted something bitter. I had forgotten to mention the grocery store encounter with Evan to Stacy.

down. He asked me to go with him to the diner."

Stacy's gaze instantly shifted from intrigued to understanding and sympathetic. She understood how the diner had always held a soft spot in my heart after our mom had passed. It was similar to the way that the motel felt like a piece of our father. Some places were just built more from memories than wood and stone.

We looked at each other between sugary bites of brightly colored candy. There weren't any words to mend the wounds in our broken hearts after losing both of our parents, so close together. However, sometimes it was okay to not have all of the words.

Stacy pinched the plastic sides of the tiny package and shook it above my hand. The last pink jelly bean tumbled into my hand as her eyes longingly watched it like a hawk observing prey from the sky.

I quickly added, "You can have it. I know it's your favorite."

Stacy simply shrugged and added, "But I want you to have it."

"Thanks, Stacy."

"Don't mention it. I still need ice."

entryway that suddenly grew a little less private as the front door opened and two rough housing twins tumbled into the foyer. I gave a barely perceptible side-eyed glance to Stacy as I handed her the ice pack and a glass of water.

"Thanks, what were you trying to tell me earlier?"

I absently waved around my head in an attempt to momentarily derail the conversation. The mother of the two terror-twins smiled and waved as one of the twins arched his head back like a snake and sank his teeth into the upper arm of his sibling. A long keening cry reverberated around the hallway as the brother remained momentarily latched onto his sibling's appendage like a crocodile right before it prepared to death-roll.

Horrified, I prepared to intervene, but a sickly sweet voice rang out from near the top of the stairs, "Kids, if you're going to fight like that then at least go outside to play. Remember what you already did to the rug near the front door?"

thumped closed. The kids momentarily stared at each other like owls until the one still caught in a slobbery death-grip head-butted his captor and then scampered back outside.

Eventually, Stacy leaned over and asked, "What happened to the front door rug?"

I involuntarily winced, "Beats me. I'll look at it later. We can't kick them out. We still need their money if we are going to have even the slightest chance at being able to break even this week."

Stacy shivered as a brisk wind from the opened front door whirled into the room. She muttered just under her breath, "Those kids are such a handful."

"Blame their wrangler. I think she's given up."

"They're about seven. That's pretty early to admit defeat."

"I wouldn't know, Stacy. Having a pet fish is as much upkeep and maintenance as I'm willing to do at the moment."

"Mr. Bubbles, died last week."

and then opened it again like a fish gasping for air.

Stacy caught the motion and said, "No, Mr. Bubbles didn't die from asphyxiation. He was a fish. I'm pretty sure that he died from obesity. It looked like you overfed him. The tiny rocks were covered with food. I didn't tell you that he died because I thought that you already knew!"

I covered my face with the palm of my hand and then dragged it down to my chin. Not even a goldfish was safe from my nefarious clutches.

"I'm a murderer, Stacy!"

"No. I'm pretty sure that you were just being an enabler to a fish that liked to eat too much. You know, I read somewhere that goldfish will just keep eating even if their tummies are full. Apparently, they don't have a good grasp on hunger so in all seriousness, he probably died from too many fish flakes."

"Thanks, Stacy. That makes me feel so much better."

"It's a little bit better that Mr. Bubbles was a goldfish and not a kid."

"Stacy?"

"I thought so."

Stacy hummed in the back of her throat and added, "Tell me about the phone call. It's obvious that you'll have to clear a few things up with Evan. Even if you just want to be friends, it's only fair that you're able to communicate with him. Jeffrey always makes it a point to talk to me when there is even the smallest chance that we aren't on the same page. It's not so much about having different opinions and it's more about making sure that there isn't any confusion along the way."

For a younger sister, Stacy did have a fairly sturdy grasp on the relationship essentials. Not that I needed or could afford a talk about that given the current state of the motel. I tossed my head back and sighed, "Let's talk in the kitchen. I need to tell you about the phone call and you're probably not going to like it."

"On a positive note, this can bring more business. On a slightly less positive note, I am pretty sure that we could go to jail for this, or at the very least have the reputation of the motel permanently ruined."

"Thanks, Stacy. I hadn't thought of all of these horrible consequences before." I defensively folded my arms across my chest and pulled my flannel shirt tighter with the motion. The pesky cotton material crumpled and folded awkwardly along my chest, but for once the awkward motion didn't bother me. It was too low on my priority list to matter.

"I don't want to scare you! Maybe this can be a good thing for us. You only put the story online with the very best intentions. Besides, who knew that people would actually look at that advertisement? The internet is all so new and random."

"That's what I get for putting something out there after too much wine. This is just so problematic."

"Don't say that, Lacy. We are all in this together. Now, we need to find a way to make this work. This building is really old. Strange things are definitely friendly kind from the kid's movies. Lilacs!"

Stacy always had a way with words. She hated cursing and usually just replaced actual swear words with the names of flowers. Her constantly sunny personality helped to lessen the tension.

I tried my best not to roll my eyes for the hundredth time this week since she had started mentioning a possible supernatural encounter. I spoke in a deadpanned voice and countered, "Ghosts aren't real."

"This isn't a time to be a nonbeliever, Lacy."

"You're right. I'll go back to the library and see what I can find about this place."

Loud commotion from the upper level momentarily took my attention away from our conversation in the kitchen.

Stacy mumbled, "How did they get back inside?"

"Maybe the twins are really the ghouls of this place."

Stacy gave me a bemused smile as she warned, "Careful, their mom could hear you."

back. I'm pretty sure we will need to spend more than it's worth just to clean up the arts and crafts sparkles that they tossed down the hallway this morning."

A mental image of two baby elephants clomping around upstairs popped into my mind. How did they have so much energy?

I fleetingly wondered if I could trade with the two pint-sized demons and just scare the potential film crew away with all of their tiny diabolical enthusiasm. A loud crash rang from the floor above as a tiny high-pitched voice yelped, "That sounds expensive."

A deranged part of me wanted to stomp up the stairs and investigate the damage. However, a more mature sliver of rationality held the reins and insisted that I stay downstairs. I knew that my temper at the moment wouldn't be the best. The kids were definitely annoying, but that didn't mean that they deserved to be scared to death.

As if I had said every single thought out loud, Stacy agreed, "No need to look. Let's just make some hot chocolate and plan how we can find a few real haunting stories about this place."

"Let's not push out luck. We're only in the early 2000s."

"Lamb chops? Since when does Jeffrey cook lamb chops for the guests? Sounds delicious. Expensive, but delicious."

Two days after talking with Stacy, I had finally ventured out into town. In theory, the scent of spaghetti and the taste of actually real ripe produce was supposed to be a welcome change of pace. We usually stuck to canned vegetables in order to keep the costs low, so this was a special treat.

I looked at the different cuts of lamb and sighed. Several pounds later, I rolled my grocery cart into the next aisle. A loud crash erupted from the cart and my hands wobbled on the handle as I looked around confused. How did I hit the corner of the aisle?

Grocery list in hand, I looked up and nearly rolled my eyes at the irony. Of course, the one person in town that I wanted to hide from was the one person that it seemed like I couldn't avoid.

"Hi, Evan. Sorry about the little grocery cart fender bender. I was distracted and driving."

temperature outside that had only moments ago attacked his exposed skin. Each day seemed colder than the last so it only stood to reason that Evan didn't fare well in the cold.

"Hey, Lacy. No worries. I won't ask for your license and registration." He awkwardly shuffled his weight from one leg to the other and glanced away.

Stupid. Stupid. He's not cold! His face is red because he's embarrassed. The realization hit my chest with the subtlety of a sledgehammer.

"Do you want to go to the library with me?" The sentence broke free and escaped into the shopping aisle. I watched the invisible sound waves in horror as they spun around the tooth brushes and tampons and smacked right into Evan's ears. So much for tactful.

His brows furrowed as he tilted his head to the right in an ever so subtle manner. Evan reached up and rubbed the back of his neck, "That could work. Do you need something specific?"

Now it was my turn to be honest. I shook my head no and explained, "I need to find some information

Evan effectively removed his cart out of the grate of my own little yellow cart and walked closer to the tooth brushes. I couldn't see his face as he turned to the side and asked, "Do you want my help looking?"

"I would like some company when searching through the records. The information is most likely in the basement of the library and that place looks like it hasn't been touched since the Vietnam War."

Evan snorted as he plucked a blue toothbrush from the rack and placed the weight of his full gaze on my face. He agreed, "That sounds like an adventure. Let's go. You can tell me all about your sudden interest in ancient records on the way over."

"Perfect. I'll drive."

"I didn't expect anything less."

"Maggie Smith, adores you." Evan chuckled as he walked down the old creaky stairs.

"I really hope that's true. We bonded over a love of older newspaper articles and the importance of the now rarely used Dewey Decimal System." I absently placed a wayward strand of hair behind my ear and looked around the library basement.

From the corner of my eye, I watched as Evan's lips turned upward into the faintest hint of a smile. He glanced at the side of my face and then quickly clapped his hands together before he walked deeper into the chaotically organized bookshelves. Thick layers of dust coated the books in what could only be described as grime. Even the fake plant in the corner had lost its green plastic vigor and metaphorically grown wilted over time as fine particles of old paper eventually fell from the air and weighed down the leaves.

Evan attempted to retrieve a book from one of the top shelves. I watched in horror as the accident happened in slow motion. The shelf wasn't steady and the slight movement jostled the other books free from assaulted Evan's nose.

A startled groan left his lips as I anxiously sped through the haze of dust like a car on a dark stormy night. The cloud of dander and grime eventually settled enough so that I could find Evan and inspect the damage.

My brows pressed together in a hard line as I concentrated on the wound. A spot of blood crept from the corner of his injured lip and marred the previously perfect skin.

"You're hurt."

"Where?"

I leaned up onto the tips of my toes and winced. The corner of his lip had split thanks to the pointy end of an outdated World Almanac from 1956. In all honesty, the damage could have been worse if the massive book had hit him even a few inches closer to his eye. I stood on the tips of my toes and reached out my hand. My thumb carefully caressed the corner of Evan's mouth and removed the speck of blood. The wound didn't look so bad under the dim shaky overhead light bulbs.

A sudden wave of awareness crashed against my mind as a violently pulled me back to reality. I coughed

"You'll live."

After a second, I added, "Wrong shelf, Evan. I'll just stack the fallen books in the corner and we can try and fix the shelf before we leave."

Eager for a distraction, I quickly plucked a few heavy books from the floor and hefted the weight against my hip. I placed a few books on the top of a wooden desk near the front corner of the basement. A tingling in the back of my nose threw me into a sneezing fit. I sneezed so hard that my eyes started to water.

Evan pulled out a miniature packet of tissues as he held five heavy duty novels grasped firmly within one hand. He added them to the stack and then looked around the basement and sighed.

"Do you know what are we looking for in this pile? A treasure map? The deed to a long-forgotten family treasure? The Declaration of Independence?"

I scuffed the toe of my black boot into the concrete and tried to find a way to stall. There wasn't a fair way to talk around the elephant in the room.

Finally, I shoved my hands deep into the tiny back pocket of my jeans and absently searched the

My lips felt chapped as I carefully weighed my next words, "We need to find out more about the history of the motel. In all reality my dad named it a motel, but it's more like a Bed and Breakfast. It never felt right to change the name in order to fit the technicality. I'm rambling. Stacy and I really need to find a reason to potentially perhaps believe that the motel is haunted."

Evan narrowed his eyes at me and parroted, "Potentially perhaps believe that it's haunted?"

"It's a bit complicated, but I need to see if there are any records in the town paper about the motel. It was originally a massive home for a wealthy family. Apparently, the family that built the home came from a long line on the East Coast."

"We're basically on the East Coast."

I struggled, but luckily succeeded in holding in my eye roll. Instead, I quipped, "Further East, Evan. Think like New York and Vermont. We're getting distracted. The point is I need to find information about the motel."

Evan nodded along, "Okay, so you told me the goal. Now is there a specific reason that we are tucked specific reason that you need to find this information so quickly?"

He was fishing for information. Unfortunately, I wasn't in the mood to take the bait. Even if Evan was an extremely attractive stranger.

My chest pinched with the slightest squeeze of regret. Evan hadn't given me a single reason to distrust him. In all honesty, Evan had actually gone above and beyond to accommodate and befriend me. In any other situation, I would have pulled out two chairs and sang away about my reasoning, but there was just too much at stake. Stacy and Jeffrey would be out on the streets if I didn't play this close to the vest and properly clean up my own mess. Everything had to be spotless so I didn't want to risk giving Evan even the smallest hint of crumbs. I already felt like I had said too much.

Worse, the television crew was coming to the motel before the end of the year. With less than a month to prepare for their arrival, it felt like the walls were slowly creeping in on me with every consistent tick of the clock.

puddle of panic. I usually felt like a strong combination of both. Sometimes I fantasized about leaving the motel in the middle of the night and getting an accounting job in the big city. As if accounting firms hired at three in the morning. My nerves were most definitely shot after so many months of just trying to survive.

Instead, I learned to make lists as a way to cope. The list for today had insisted that I head to the library for information. Several hours later, the visit was now a potential disaster. Why had I asked Evan to come?

As if he could read the indecision on my face, Evan lowered his shoulders and looked like a slightly deflated balloon. He tilted his head to the side and admitted, "It's okay. You don't need to tell me anything if it feels too personal. You can tell me when and if you're ready."

A small smile of relief lit up my features as I added, "You're pretty confident that you'll win me over. What if I never tell?"

"In any situation, confidence is key. Especially, when the situation involves a very gorgeous woman. I'm not saying that this has anything to do with the current

For someone so potentially imposing, he managed to have a gentleness around him wherever he went. It was like a breath of fresh air whenever he walked into a room. He brought an odd sense of sunshine combined with wit and kindness.

"We will see, Casanova. Now, help me find where they stashed all of the older newspapers."

"Sure. Do you have a light?"

"I don't think that you can smoke down here. This is an ancient wooden building, after all."

"No, Lacy. I mean do you have a flashlight?"

My pride wouldn't allow me to answer. Instead, I fished around in my pockets and pulled out my cell phone. I flicked on the screen and began to explore the darker corners of the basement where the sparse light bulbs weren't strong enough to fully push away the darkness.

From a few paces behind my back, I heard, "Phones. I should have thought of that."

I didn't say anything, but a faint smirk tipped the corner of my lip upward in satisfaction. It was a childish

In the distance, an object flickered against the beams of my makeshift torch. It wasn't an overpowering shimmer, but it was just enough to draw my attention. I inched closer and realized that the floorboards dipped lower, the further that I crept.

Evan grumbled, "Leave it to the librarian to put all of the ambiguous information in such an out of the way location."

"What's wrong? Are you scared of small spaces?"

A sudden lull in the conversation told me everything that I needed to know as Evan sucked in a deep breath of air from between his teeth. He sounded like an angry pet gerbil, but I kept that tidbit of information to myself. There was no point in upsetting the only person in town that had been outrageously kind to me. It was an odd situation, but it wasn't every day that I needed to wander under the underbelly of an ancient library and squeeze into spaces two sizes too small for a normal human.

uncomfortable position.

Evan's footsteps had halted a few minutes ago, but he angled his light in my direction so that it was easier for me to see what was up ahead. I sent a silent prayer to up above for whoever or whatever was listening. This wasn't the time for a rogue mouse to scamper over my feet. The ceiling was too low so I was stuck between a stressed crawl and a haphazard crouch in order to reach the mysterious object.

Finally, I was close enough so that I could reach out and grab it. My fingers touched cool solid metal and I realized that it was a small box. Upon closer inspection, I noticed that it had an inscription carved into a silver nameplate. My fingers absently traced over the material as I sounded out the words, "Ms. Lockwood's safe."

For a moment, I wasn't sure what to do with such an odd object. It was much too small to hold an entire newspaper so a large part of me wanted to just put it back and continue on with the search. However, a very small and persistent part of me decided to open the box.

"Well, that's inconvenient."

"Lacy? What did you find?"

"It looks like a box that was left here for safekeeping. It must be over a hundred years old!"

Evan whistled in the back of his throat as he enthusiastically waved around his phone. The action bounced the beams of light off of the walls and sent the room and pipes spinning in a flurry of white.

I laughed, "Evan, hold the light steady. It's hard enough to see in this cramped corner."

"Sure."

"Thank you."

The light suddenly grew steady as it landed on the silver box within my palms. I couldn't tell if the substantial amount of weight within my arms came from the actual metallic box or from its contents.

I nibbled my lower lip and weighed my options. I wanted to be able to look inside, but it felt wrong to steal something so interesting from the library. However, it wasn't really stealing if nobody even knew to look for it. Besides, the heavy layer of dust and intricate craftsmanship pointed out that it had most definitely

My back inched into Evan's beam of light as my arms were hidden in the shadows. I placed the little box inside of my coat. Satisfied, I half-crawled and half-shimmied back into the larger part of the basement. It would be my tiny little secret.

After an hour of searching, I decided that it was about time to give up or at least take a break. I didn't want to throw away the rest of the afternoon looking for documents that had possibly turned into a pile of ashes over several decades ago. Deflated, I itched the top of my nose and peered at my folded jacket that sneakily hid the tiny metallic box.

Suddenly, Evan called, "Lacy! Look at this!"

"Coming!"

My feet sprung into action as I weaved my way around the bookcases until I spotted Evan crouched on the floor next to a stack of randomly strewn papers. He picked up a small pile of items with a youthful amount of excitement.

Evan murmured, "There are also a few old slides that can fit in an old-fashioned projector. I have a feeling that the much older documents were switched over to the projector right before the fire. If so, we're in luck."

"That's a great idea, Evan. I'll find the ancient projector and we can try out one of the slides."

"Easy, I accidentally sneezed on it only a few minutes ago. This is one of those rare times in life when I'm happy to be allergic to dust."

Evan snickered as he went to work and collected a few of the older slides from the pile. The dates were vaguely written on the top of the objects, but luckily the marks were still somewhat legible.

I returned with a circular object in tow. It felt heavier than I had expected, but I didn't mind as I swiftly set it up and prepared to insert a slide.

"Are you sure that this is a projector?"

"Yep. It's a little on the round side. It's called a carousel projector and the slides move in a circular pattern. Let's just hope that it works after all of these years."

Evan nodded and handed me several slides as he mumbled, "Fingers crossed."

It took me a moment to figure out the design, but the projector whirred to life as a black and white image projected into the room and landed on the concrete wall. The light creme color of the cement created the perfect makeshift background for the images. The images

Upon closer inspection, I realized that the specific article headline dated back to the late 1800s. A thrill of excitement whirled down my spine. After countless hours of searching for clues, it finally felt like we were headed in the right direction. I absently reached out my arm and squeezed Evan's hand in a combination of elation and fear.

A million questions raced around my brain as I struggled to read the title of the headline and fully grasp the meaning of the content. The jargon felt outdated, but the message still read the same as it had over one hundred and some years ago. Apparently, the town had experienced a scandal that related to a defamed newspaper writer and a young town socialite. The content looked interesting, but I only skimmed the article as it clearly had nothing to do with the old motel.

I impatiently moved through a few slides and tapped my heel against the concrete floor as a deep sense of dissatisfaction crept over my body. It was almost like with each slide that passed, we were one step closer to discovering the history of the Mistletoe Motel.

supernatural fanatics and ghost chasers. It wasn't too hard to talk the pretend skeptics and steadfast believers into a haunting, but something told me that an entire camera crew devoted to finding ghosts was an entirely different ballgame. At this point, we were still playing foosball, but we really needed to play actual soccer. It didn't look like the motel stood a chance against the professionals.

Worse, the lie would surely ruin my sister's reputation. A deep sense of shame bubbled up from my stomach and threatened to pour out onto the cold black basement floor. It tasted bitter and sharp against the back of my throat and tongue.

One tiny story about an old person living a long healthy life and then passing away was all that I needed. Darkly, I pondered if it was possible to claim that my own parents haunted the halls of the motel. The situation looked pretty desperate and the slides didn't talk about a single ancient person passing away in the home. At this point, any mention of the motel felt like a slim bet.

"Stop!"

"What's wrong, Evan?"

"Go back and look at the last slide."

My fingers whirled into overdrive as I held my breath. A white outline of a regal Victorian building met my curious gaze. I reread the title of the newspaper article for a third time without any success in understanding the meaning. It just felt too surreal.

"Impossible."

"This definitely counts for a bit of unexpected history."
Evan stood from his previously seated position on an old
discarded wooden desk.

Specks of dirt and dust whirled around in the air
like miniature temperamental airplanes with no intention
of calmly landing on the ground. Each particle flew
through the air and only became visible when
illuminated by the beams of light that pierced the
previously dark veil of ignorance. The dust was likely
also right next to my face, but I could only see the flecks
caught mid-dive-bomb through the luster of antiquated
projector light.

Evan ambled over to the wall and his shadow
spread from his back and expanded along the room until
it almost appeared like he had two black wings. My
research companion looked similar to a brooding
avenging angel as he rubbed away a splatter of dust from
his fitted black shirt. As if the basement didn't have
enough distractions and detours to last a lifetime.

Half of me didn't want to look at what was
displayed so proudly against the wall directly next to

114

a sheet of paper on an ancient printing press and then copied onto a projector slide, any less real. The facts didn't care about my dislike or fear. They impassively remained showcased on the wall as my eyes looked them over with disdain.

I tilted my head up and focussed my gaze away from the dust so that I could see the bigger picture. My heart seemed to skip a beat as I looked up in wonder at the headline of the article.

"Local woman goes missing. Crazed fanatic suspected." A black and white picture of the motel stood in the distance as several men in sophisticated hats and suits loitered around the front yard. The steep incline that placed the house on a hill looked ominous instead of inviting.

For the first time, a shiver of trepidation crept down my spine as I looked at the picture and thought of our family motel. Did something sinister actually happen at our beloved downtrodden motel? Was Stacy just better at perceiving the truth than I was? Hundreds of questions whirled around in my mind as I tried to understand why such a story had never been spoken of around town.

and someone else's great grandma the wealthy heiress with a questionable past. Such news about the motel, even more than a hundred years later, seemed unlikely to be forgotten in the oral memory of our sleepy town.

"Lacy, can you play around with the quality of the image? We might be able to read the newspaper article and find out more."

I absently nodded my head. Evan didn't see the gesture as his eyes remained locked on the imposing image of the motel. It had to be one of the very first photographs used in a newspaper. The process must have been expensive, but for some reason the paper had deemed the story important enough to go the extra financial mile.

My fingers deftly inspected the projector in hopes of improving the quality of the image. The story needed to be brought back from the graveyard of time. There were still too many unanswered questions and possible outcomes from the past that could still potentially help the future of the motel.

"Yes!" I hissed the single word out in victory as a tiny knob on the side of the machine brought the slide block-letter words.

"Scoot. Your massive back is blocking the light." I lightly nudged Evan and his shadowy wings out of the way.

"You like my back, Lacy?"

"Move it or lose it, Buddy."

Evan chuckled and ambled just shy of the light. He turned to me as an easy smile tipped up the edges of his lips.

I walked closer to the screen and decided to read the entire story. Curiosity killed the cat.

Local young woman missing. Crazed Fanatic Suspected.

Lilian Lockwood, one of the loveliest faces this side of the Mississippi, was declared missing by her father early yesterday morning. All fingers and information point to Mr. O'Ceallaigh from the Town of Mirwood.

Mr. O'Ceallaigh originally hailed from Ireland as a portion of teaming refuse that landed upon the United States soil in search of refuge from what some people claim are harsh conditions and religious persecution.

It was known that Mr. O'Ceallaigh never attended a Sunday service in town. He worked as a writer until disgraced. Many townspeople say that they can often see him coming nearly several miles away due to his flaming red hair that stands out against the lush greenery of our town.

Neighbors of the Lockwood family agree that Mr. O'Ceallaigh took an unnatural interest in the just to catch a glimpse of her.

Mr. O'Ceallaigh is wanted by the town Sheriff and mayor. There is an award for his capture and return. His whereabouts are unknown. Wanted alive.

"That's just silly."

Evan guffawed, "A woman goes missing and you call it silly?"

"Of course. Mr. O' Ceallaigh had no reason to attend such a religious service. They said that he's Irish so that means that he was more than likely Catholic. The founders of the Mirwood town and even our own town were all Protestants. That means that the religious service wasn't for him, so why would he go? What an intentionally biased story! It makes him sound horrible and I don't even know him."

Frustrated, I tossed up my arms into the air and stalked in a tiny circle. It really irritated me that someone could write something so openly biased. Worse, it felt somewhat similar to the poor caliber of reporting often gleaned in more modern gossip papers. Yes, there were high-level merited journalists, but there were also writers that lacked spine and wrote stories solely based around shock, fear, and hatred.

After about two laps around the projector, I sighed, "It's no question who's side the newspaper and narrowed my eyes at the screen in distaste.

"I didn't even think of that. You're right. That was a pretty lousy way to mislead the entire town about this man. Did they say if he was guilty?"

Only slightly less irritated, I shook my head and added, "No. The article doesn't mention if he was taken into custody."

Evan folded his arms across his chest and looked at the black and white photo of the motel with a look of curiosity combined with disdain. He tilted his head to the side and admitted, "Thanks for reading it out loud. I forgot my reading glasses in the car. It's not fair if he was innocent, but the town definitely called it if he was guilty. The problem is you never know all of the information from outside of the problem. Heck, even people inside of a problem don't have all of the facts. I don't think we will ever really know what happened to this poor Lilian lady."

I shrugged my shoulders and stared completely entranced by the image of the motel. It looked nearly exactly the same as today. It was almost as if it had successfully remained untouched by time.

probably got the brunt of a bunch of unnecessary harshness because he was technically viewed as a different religion. It makes me wonder how much has really changed since then."

"That's a pretty grim assessment, Lacy."

"Maybe, but it doesn't feel wrong."

"Well, maybe Lilian ended up being found. It's possible that she had fallen off of her horse or ended up lost. It wasn't exactly like they had cell phones or even email back then."

"That is something to think about, too."

My shadow momentarily blocked out the light from the projector as I crossed the distance to the other side of the massive basement. I playfully nudged Evan's side with my hip and sent him playful wave. The action helped to lessen the serious mood.

I looked back at the screen, partially mesmerized and admitted, "That's why I like numbers."

Evan furrowed his thick brows and asked, "What?"

"Before the motel, I was supposed to be an accountant. I love numbers because they don't lie. There everyone speaks and we all adhere to the rules even if we don't realize it. Think about it. Numbers are like this strange universal language where everything has an order."

"That's an oddly romantic train of thought for someone that runs in the opposite direction at the slightest display of human emotion."

"Hey, you don't know that about me. I will let you know that I am really great to my sister." I folded my arms over my chest as I felt somewhat defensive.

"We both know that you're trying to change the topic by bringing your sister into this. You know exactly what I am talking about." He arched a knowing eyebrow in my direction.

It's true. I knew exactly what Evan was talking about, but that didn't mean I was about to admit it. Instead, I gave him the slightest tilt of my head as a form of silent admission.

My mind drifted back to the article illuminated against the cold rough basement wall. The entire story sounded slightly fishy to me. I couldn't put my finger on it, but something just felt out of place. The story was had originally started as a single-family home. Now, I finally had solid proof. The motel had first been owned and built by the Lockwood family.

A slight shiver crept up my spine as the chill within the frigid room finally seeped into my body. Maybe the unsettling newspaper story hadn't helped in that area. I rubbed my hands up and down my arms and tried to create a small amount of friction.

Evan glanced down and muttered something unintelligible as he stalked to another area of the room. Within a few seconds, he returned with his own thick jacket that he had removed earlier in the day.

"Here. You'll be no use to the motel if you catch a cold."

"Thanks, Evan." I accepted the jacket and slipped it over my arms. It looked several sizes too big, but it definitely did the trick. The small hairs on my arms seemed to calm down as the goose pimples on my neck slowly faded away.

"Let's get out of here, Evan."

basement."

I reached out and patted his arm, "Thanks for being a good sport about it."

I didn't have the heart to point out that between the two of us, I was the only one that had crawled into the smallest corners of the room. My mind wandered to the tiny metallic box that was still hidden underneath my coat. I hadn't even realized how close Evan had come to discovering the small box until he had kindly brought me his own jacket. Maybe luck was on my side. If so, I intended to make the most of such a rare occasion.

Two sets of feet headed up the wooden library stairs and stopped on the first level landing in the back of the building. For a moment, Evan's chest remained pressed against my back as we both paused. Our now light sensitive eyes adjusted to the bright afternoon sun that poured through the large glass windows. I slowly looked up and the droll sounds from the library slowly faded into the background as Evan's observant blue orbs clashed with my curious gaze.

Suddenly, I leaned up an inch, but just as quickly decided against it. What would the town think about

125

against my ribs. Absently, my arms flexed and pressed the sharp corner against my stomach.

Suddenly, I recognized a face that I hadn't seen in ages. My eyes snapped to Anna as she sat at one of the tables in the middle of the library and tapped an old pencil against her pink colored lips. She casually popped a bubble between her lips as if on autopilot. Our eyes locked in an impromptu staring contest. Eventually, she blinked. I noticed a new book as it sat untouched on the top of the wooden desk. It looked as if she had just arrived.

I wasn't sure what to do after so many years without talking to people outside of the motel. Anna had been one of my closest friends before everything had crumbled.

Unannounced, Maggie hustled out from one of the stacks. She looked like a woman on a mission as she headed in Anna's direction like a missile to a heat signal. Her crows feet seemed more pronounced as she scrunched up her eyes while Anna snapped another large bubble and then proceeded to chew almost as loudly as a cow chewing cud. I nibbled my lower lip and waved back to her original task.

Anna's eyes looked like saucers as Maggie whispered out, "No gum in the library. Especially, when you're popping bubbles. Don't make me tell your mom about this at our poker game tonight."

Poker games. That's right. Mid-week poker games were about as chaotic as our sleepy town got. The older ladies dressed like it was their night at the opera. They usually took turns and moved the game to a different home each week. They used to come to the motel at least once a month for a game, but the gaggle of women had stopped after my parents had passed away. In all honesty, I hadn't bothered to invite them back.

I sent a quick wave over to Anna and then quickly walked to the exit. As far as reintroductions go, I was sure that this wasn't my best work.

Meeting people from town felt like turning the page in a book that I just wasn't ready to leave. I didn't want to move onto the next chapter because deep down I was afraid of what was written in the rest of the book. Not going to poker night and staying at the motel was

I had always wanted to join the poker group on the premise of counting cards, but I worried that it would look odd to be the youngest player by twenty to thirty years. Instead, I often contented myself with the occasional story from Letty as she rang up the motel groceries.

I pulled away from my jumbled poker thoughts and struggled to keep in a laugh at the tiny chaotic drama of our town.

How could a woman go missing without a trace when people couldn't even chew gum in the library without being detected and firmly scolded? The story stuck in the back of my mind like a nest of angry bees. The thought swarmed around at a dizzying pace and remained just out of reach.

The rusted paint of the library doors stood out against the multi-colored afternoon light. We had been in the library for more than a few hours, but at least we now had at least one solid clue. There was definitely an undiscovered mystery associated with the hotel and it was real.

impending arrival of the television crew loomed in the distance like an ominous warning sign.

I rearranged the stolen treasure wrapped with my jacket and then grunted. The action reanimated my previously dead tired muscles as I hurried back to the car. For once, my mind was too busy with possible outcomes about the newspaper story. I didn't care about my list of impending daily chores.

Exhausted, I looked down and avoided the cracks in the concrete. I wanted something to hold my scattered attention. The action felt childish, but also extremely freeing as my feet actively avoided a trail of cracks in the old concrete parking lot.

A deep chuckle from a few feet behind, told me that Evan was also headed on his way out. We walked in silence for a few seconds before he leisurely drawled, "You know that you drove both of us here, right?"

His tone sounded half-playful and half-taunting. Darn him.

A near crimson blush crept along the nape of my neck, but luckily it was hidden underneath Evan's thick wool collared jacket. He was right. Instead of mumbling

So much for a stroke of luck.

"Do you want to tell me the real reason that we scrounged around the bottom of a basement all afternoon? I know that I said that I wouldn't bug you for an answer, but that newspaper story made me curious. Not that I mind if searching through the archives is what you secretly like to do for fun."

Evan fiddled with the seatbelt as it jammed for the third time and refused to cross his broad shoulders. He grunted and tried a fourth time and the temperamental belt mercifully obliged.

I watched the fight from the corner of my eye and prepared to leave the library parking lot. It wasn't a long drive back to the supermarket, but the roads were slick with a combination of rain and ice from the day before. The conditions weren't ideal so the ride would take longer than normal. Apparently, I had accidentally trapped myself into a relatively uncomfortable situation. I carefully weighed my words and decided that Evan wouldn't try to hurt the motel with information. It also didn't hurt that he had spent the majority of the day playing amateur detective with some of the oldest curiosity. Only some.

"This is completely off the books."

"Deal. Whatever you tell me, it doesn't leave this car. I promise." Evan's voice held a stern quality that bordered on a resolution.

The stray nervous butterflies at the bottom of my tummy fluttered around in anticipation of my next sentence. I watched the road as trees moved in a blur of dark greens and browns. My foot gently pressed against the brake pedal in anticipation of a blind curve. The road quickly snapped at an angle that resembled a rubber band as it rushed back into place. Years of practice taught my muscles how to hit the curve at just the perfect speed and angle in the old questionable-at-best truck. The worn brake pads squealed in protest and Evan winced at the harsh sound. Well, it was either the disks or the brakes, but either way it wasn't good. The mechanic in him was probably dying to say something, but to his credit, he refrained.

Now it was my turn to fill the silence. I ran the tip of my tongue along the outside of my teeth as if tasting how the ghostly lie about the motel had tainted seats assaulted my nose. The faintest traces of a caramel that I had popped into my mouth before entering the supermarket remained firm in one of my shark teeth and I internally cringed. There was no way that such a horrible lie could taste like the last remaining traces of a caramel square.

I gathered my thoughts and answered, "The motel was in the red. Well, the motel is still in the red, but it's much closer to breaking even than before. It looked like we weren't even going to make it to Christmas. It was bad. One night, I had a bottle of wine and decided to watch a little television. One thing led to another and then suddenly we had customers at the motel. They all claimed that they were interested in staying at the haunted Mistletoe Motel. I guess the motel had haunted me financially more than I had admitted. After a few supernatural television shows, I suppose the two thoughts ended up mushed together online."

I paused and decided if I wanted to admit the full truth, "My dad."

That was all that I could manage. Slightly dejected, I pivoted the conversation and continued, "In from so I really am scrambling to justify it. In all honesty, I'm not even sure how I managed to put anything on the internet. Everything that happened is completely my fault and my sister and Jeffrey have nothing to do with this mess. I made a massive disaster and I'm really trying to fix it. It feels like all I ever do is make massive mistakes. It's so frustrating to never feel like I'm making progress. It's always backwards and for once, I have this chance to get ahead, but it's all because of the wrong reasons."

Evan reached across the center console and placed a comforting palm against my shoulder as he whispered, "You're not a mess. It's just a bad position. You don't go into the city when you want to see the stars shine at night. You need to get out of the city in order to get a better perspective. It's not as bad as it sounds. Take a step back and look at it from a different perspective."

I chuckled without an ounce of humor and countered, "You're right. It's much worse. That popular ghost hunting television show called and said that they want to stay at the motel for a weekend. I couldn't think of an excuse to say no. The crew will be here the

It took us all day just to find an ominous and inconclusive newspaper clipping."

My voice sounded tense and strained. It just felt like an uphill battle and even my throat knew it.

Evan remained silent as he digested everything that I had just told him. His fingers tapped against the lip of the rolled-up passenger window. It was too chilly to keep it rolled down so the car felt exponentially smaller with the glass effectively trapping us together.

He released a low sigh and then slapped his opened palm against his muscular thigh. Evan acted as if he had just made a personal decision on the matter.

"Well, the next step is to go back online. Let's go all out and see what we can find about the motel. Two heads are better than one. Luckily, it looks like you have three when we count Stacy and Jeffrey. Count me in." An excited grin broadened his features as his blue eyes danced with excitement.

I found his excitement infectious and soon felt a large grin on my own face as it stretched from one cheek to the other. The clouds of uncertainty had blown out to sea and left nothing, but a sunny day filled with hope in

"I think that I'm going to be sick."

"You've already said that twice, Stacy. Go upstairs and burn some sage for a little. We still have some time to turn this around."

Stacy turned her sharp feminine features in my direction and fluttered her lengthy eyelashes at me in incredulity. She stuck her pert nose up into the air in defiance, but pivoted with the grace of a ballerina as she quickly headed up the stairs. Her voice rang down the hall as she called, "I'll also cleanse your room!"

"No!" The harsh cry echoed off the walls and Stacy froze with one foot floating between the step and the ground.

Quickly, I tried to cover up my own mistake, "No, thank you, Stacy. You already work so hard and we really need to clean that room upstairs once that couple checks out at noon."

Stacy slowly lowered her foot onto the wooden step as her still somewhat startled gaze rested on my face. A wave of guilt rocked the boat of my already roiled conscience. The last thing that I wanted was to be television show would metaphorically start sinking my already precariously positioned mental health boat. It was one thing to weather a storm, but another beast to survive a sinking ship.

"I'm sorry for snapping at you, Stacy. The ghost hunting crew really has me on edge. That's no excuse. Please, I'll just handle my room right now. It's a bit chaotic. Besides, you shouldn't have to do that on your birthday."

From the somewhat unreadable expression on Stacy's face, I could tell that she didn't believe my words, but also didn't want to push the subject. Finally, she shrugged her shoulders and agreed, "Fine. No sage for you."

Before she completely disappeared from view, she called, "Have you seen my lucky lighter? I left it in my dresser last night, but I haven't been able to find it."

"No, but I'll look around."

Stacy joked, "Where? In my room?"

"No, silly. I'll look around down here."

"You won't find it downstairs."

"Why not?"

"Even a better reason to find it. Don't worry, I'm sure it will turn up before your birthday dinner."

Stacy popped her hip to the side and placed a slim hand against her hip as she asked, "Oh, really? How do you know that?"

I wiggled my eyebrows and waved my arms above my head as I teased, "We have the spirit world on our side. Ask and we shall receive."

"Very funny. I'll be upstairs only keeping up with the good spirits."

Yes, the ghost hunting team had me in a panic, but it wasn't the full reason that I had snapped at Stacy. In reality, the stolen metallic case from the library was still plopped right in the middle of my bed and positioned right next to a printed out article that explained the three easiest ways to pick a lock.

Talk about incriminating.

The last thing that I wanted was for my sister to know that I was not only lying to the entire nation about the motel, but had also become a possible kleptomaniac for old and unusual items. Apparently, the bad behavior was just seeping out of the ground of my tainted moral wanted to hide from Stacy.

Now, I'm sure that she just thought that I was being an ultimate jerk. I sighed and decided to make some time during the week to go into town and buy her a new CD as an apology gift slash to thank her for tolerating everything that I had dragged her into. Maybe that needed two CDs?

The disheveled living room pillows grated on my already thin nerves. I walked over and began to fluff them back into their original or at least close-to-original-as-possible position. A spasm of pain rang from the palm of my hand and seared all the way into my shoulder.

Startled, I pulled back the pillows and inspected what could possibly be so firm within the stacks of well-worn fabric. A tiny silver object peaked out from the cracks between the sofa cushions and the base. My relatively thin eyebrows nearly pressed together as I tentatively stuck my hand down into the hole and hoped for the best. The metal felt cool and icy against the skin of my sore palm. Once the item was exposed to the sunlight, I nearly gasped in shock. A sturdy metallic

"Impossible."

I tried to reason that Stacy was just being forgetful. It was possible that she had placed the lighter inside of her back pocket and that the lighter had fallen into the cracks of the sofa when she had sat down. There were several perfectly logical explanations, but none of them managed to lessen the startled hairs on the back of my neck as a cold breeze suddenly wafted into the room. The sudden change in temperature nearly sent me running as I glanced around for an open window. However, my handy moved an inch due to the lack of circulation in the room. I narrowed my eyes in skepticism and crept closer to the paneled glass.

A loud slam startled a scream from the back of my throat. I gripped the lighter so tightly in my palm that I'm sure that the engraved letters on the lighter managed to stamp into my skin.

The window farthest to the right swung open and closed, but there wasn't the faintest hint of a detectable breeze. I cupped my throat as the window eagerly swung in an untraceable wind. Just as quickly as the incident occurred, the window slammed back into night instead of safely bundled inside of our once cheery communal living room. Not trusting my eyes, I listened with everything that I had and searched for even the faintest of sounds. There had to be a perfectly logical explanation, right?

Unsteady feet trampled into the living room and I knew who it was without even needing to turn around. The floorboards creaked and complained from the excess weight as Jeffrey tumbled out of the kitchen and stampeded into the living room.

He quickly entered the room and hollered, "Not on my watch!"

I turned around as Jeffrey entered the room with a spatula in one hand and a motorized mixer in the other. He looked like an avenging Michelin star chef as his arms flexed with muscles gained from countless hours of kneading bread and tenderizing meat.

There was a brief pause before I gathered my thoughts and teased, "What were you going to do? Mix an intruder to death?"

"I didn't want to hurt anyone."

"Saved by the pacifist."

room for danger.

"You're the only person in this motel with an infinite amount of actual murder weapons and you chose to bring two different ways to mix dough instead of a pointy object like a knife?"

Instead of bothering to reply, Jeffrey lowered both the spatula and chorded mixer as he narrowed his gaze and suspiciously inspected the empty room. Satisfied, he pursed his lips and asked, "Why did you scream?"

"Because I just got the utilities bill?" Even to my own ears, it sounded more like a question.

Jeffrey rolled his eyes until only the whites were visible as he countered, "No you didn't. That comes on the tenth."

"How would you know?"

"Because you mumble about how everyone leaves the lights on and wastes water for the rest of the day. You're like clockwork, but in a good way."

Jeffrey was completely right. Not only was I completely predictable, but I was also a horrible liar. I

Slowly, Jeffrey looked in the direction of the massive windows and raised both mixing devices above his head as he crept closer. I stood taller and tried to make myself look more intimidating, just in case there really was another presence in the room. Like a raccoon or some other poor trapped critter. Not a spirit.

The window farthest away from us opened in a hurry as if a massive gust of wind had blown in from the outside elements at full speed. Just as suddenly, the window snapped shut.

Jeffrey raised the mechanical mixer into the air like a battle axe as the electric cord coiled around his legs. Each step brought him closer to the floor as the cord grew more tangled and strained.

Two steps later, Jeffrey tumbled to the ground in a fit of limbs and angles. Horrified, I sprinted over to Jeffrey and ripped the cord away from his legs as he tried to scramble away from the now possibly possessed window. We scampered and crawled out of the living room and into the main hallway as a young couple sent us a curious glance before they headed up the stairs.

Jeffrey nodded his head in agreement and muttered, "I can't tell her that this place is possessed on her birthday. That's the plot of every bad horror movie, ever."

Part of me wanted to argue with Jeffrey about his logic, but I bit down on my lip and decided against it. There was no point in arguing about the supposed supernatural with Stacy and Jeffrey. Both were committed to their belief in the other side of life, but all I cared about was getting to the other side of debt. It was as if a rock was constantly pressed against my chest and even going to bed, that rock pushed down into my belly and made it almost impossible for me to go to sleep. Hopefully, we were almost out of the danger zone.

Momentarily, my mind drifted back into the living room. What if we had traded one mortal danger for something more sinister? Had I accidentally summoned something that had always been lurking in the corners of the motel?

I gave Jeffrey a weak smile and joked, "Good. I'll help you in the kitchen."

"Please don't."

145

explained, "I think it would be safer if I cooked. Besides, don't you have a few leaky roof tiles to replace?"

He wasn't wrong. My cooking skills mainly centered around microwave food and pre-made oven pizza. Speaking of pizza.

Apparently, one miniature kitchen fire and I had instantly become exiled from helping. It was a fact that mostly hurt my pride.

"Sure. Let me just grab a bite to eat and then I'll leave you and the cooking alone."

"Sounds good."

Jeffrey lowered both mixing devices and rolled up the cord in order to avoid another clumsy ballet performance. Satisfied, he headed in the direction of the kitchen.

I shoved my hands deep into my shallow jean pockets and tried to ask in a casual manner, "Have you ever heard of something called a Veggiefresh Promise pizza?"

"What do you mean that you lost the cake?" I stood huddled next to Jeffrey in the kitchen as my nicest dress grew more wrinkled by the minute. My fingers anxiously tugged and crumpled the once immaculate hemline. We were supposed to start Stacy's surprise birthday party in less than half an hour, but the main gift had managed to evaporate into thin air. We had even invited all of the guests to attend in the living room.

Jeffrey huffed and pulled off his pink apron and tossed it onto the rack near the kitchen sink. His back was rigid as the tension from the lost cake managed to slice into his body the same way that the motel debt drilled into mine.

"Maybe one of the guests took it."

"That's definitely a possibility."

"I'll look around and try to stall Stacy. You go and find the cake."

I wiped the front on my palms down the now creased edges of the velvet dress and sighed. How could a three-layer cake possibly disappear? My heart went out to Jeffrey as he ambled out of the kitchen. He donned his all of the time that he had spent gathering ingredients. It would be horrible if it had really disappeared, or worse had been eaten by a greedy guest. Secretly, my bet was on the guests, but for once I really wanted to be wrong.

Commotion from the center hall drew my attention away from the great missing cake debacle. I walked into the living room and found an immaculately frosted white three-layered cake neatly placed on the coffee table. I subtly pinched my arm and the slight sting reminded me that I wasn't dreaming.

At a loss for words, I stared in disbelief as Evan casually mingled with a young couple that were staying at the motel. Apparently, the couple had traveled all the way from New York just to catch a glimpse of a possible supernatural Victorian ghost. I walked over to the small group that huddled near the windows. I hesitated for a moment, but then pressed on.

The kind brunette woman with her hair placed up in a messy bun, greeted, "Hi, Ms. Pondwater. The cake for your sister looks amazing! You sure move fast. I wasn't in here even less than a minute ago."

squeezed her partner's arm and sent me an excited smile that I barely managed to return.

I didn't want to make anyone believe that there was something wrong. Instead, I tried to change the topic, "Evan, I didn't know that you were coming."

His bright blonde hair looked neatly combed as a white button-up shirt demanded my attention. The clean cotton material was a sharp contrast from his usual sweaters and t-shirts. It wasn't horrible.

"I invited him." Jeffrey ambled into the room and eyed the cake the entire time that he spoke to Evan. It was safe to say Jeffrey hadn't been the one to accidentally bring the cake into the living room. If Evan found Jeffrey's behavior odd, he at least had the good sense not to mention it near the guests.

For a moment, I sent a silent threat with my eyes in Jeffrey's direction, but then I realized the futility of such an action and decided that it would just be easier to complain to him in person. Maybe later.

"What's all of this?" Stacy's voice called from the outskirts of the room.

Tears filled Stacy's eyes as she wrapped her arms around her stomach as if the action could physically hold her emotions together. The attempt failed within seconds. Fat tears poured down her cheeks as a pleased smile radiated warmth like the beams of the sun. She looked in my direction and mouthed a silent thank you.

I sent her a playful wink as Jeffrey quickly rushed to her side and wrapped her in a loving hug. They whispered sweet nothings to one another as I looked away from their private moment.

The earlier chaos long forgotten, I busied myself and prepared to serve the cake as Evan ambled over to my side and offered, "Can I help?"

"Sure. Can you please hold out the plates as I cut?"

"Sounds good."

We easily fell into a rhythm and served both Jeffrey and Stacy two very generous slices of cake. The inside of the treat looked perfectly moist and poison-free. At least, it seemed poison-free. We were all going to find out at the same time. I cautiously licked a suspicious. It didn't make sense for someone to want to poison the cake, but my questionable evening true crime binges taught me that you could never be too careful.

The last few guests patiently waited in the line to receive a slice of Jeffrey's delicious dessert. I couldn't wait to try my own slice. Luckily, it looked like there would even be room for seconds if people were so inclined. Jeffrey had really outdone himself with three entire layers.

"Thank you, Mrs. Pondwater." The younger brunette from earlier came over and thanked me.

Without thinking, I corrected, "Jeffrey was the one that made the cake. I'm no use in the kitchen. He really is the best at baking. Enjoy!"

The forced injection of excitement at the end of my sentence seemed to quell the brunette's embarrassment as she strolled back over to the sofa. I hadn't had the heart to correct her twice when she was only trying to be kind. For now, I was supposedly married due to a title mishap.

I looked around and realized that it was the first time in years that the living room had ever felt so full. A my camera and quickly snapped a photo. Lately, taking photos was at the bottom of my list, but this moment felt like an exception to the rule. I smiled and took another as the guests leisurely mingled.

"I can take a photo of you and Stacy." Evan nudged my shoulder and then added, "It's important to capture the good times."

My palms felt sweaty as I angled my head to the side and looked at his face. I cleared my throat, "That sounds perfect."

Stacy glanced in my direction and I waved her over. I gave her a firm hug and laughed at the unfamiliar sensation of hosting an event. Jeffrey really pulled everything together with a delicious cake.

"Happy birthday, Stacy. How does it feel to be twenty-two?"

"Almost the same as twenty-one. Just better. I am so happy that we were able to work the motel as a family. Whatever happens, Sis. I will always love you." Stacy gripped my hand and gave it a firm squeeze.

A ball of emotion caught in the back of my throat. I squeezed Stacy's hand in return and blinked sentimental behavior."

"Why? Are you uncomfortable?"

I parroted, "Uncomfortable?"

"You always crack jokes and ramble when you're uncomfortable."

Wow, I really needed to work on my composure. I sighed and admitted, "You're right. The jokes make me more comfortable. It helps the uncomfortable conversations bounce off a little bit easier."

"Oh. When you say uncomfortable, what you really mean is experiencing the full spectrum of human emotion." Stacy arched a defiant eyebrow.

I narrowed my eyes and wanted so badly to flick her on the side of her nose. Unfortunately, I decided I couldn't due to two important reasons. One being that it was her birthday party. Two being that there were too many witnesses.

"It's just an easier version of armor."

Instead of continuing the conversation, Stacy rolled her eyes. Her light blue shirt helped to bring out the color of her eyes. It was her lucky shirt.

"Deal."

Stacy bumped her hip against my side due to our height difference and then walked up to Evan. From a distance, I noticed how he carefully held my camera. Suddenly, he looked over and smiled in my direction.

Stacy teased just low enough for me to hear, "I'm so glad that I told Jeffrey to invite Evan."

I nearly stopped walking as I half-hissed, "I should have known it was you. Even in school, you always had a passion for playing matchmaker."

Stacy teased, "Love is a beautiful thing."

"It's just a friend-crush."

"Making up a new word doesn't change the meaning."

"Stacy, you are so annoying."

"Thanks. It's a younger sister thing."

I stuck out my tongue and pinched Lacy's hip as Evan prepared to take our photo. It was childish, but appropriate given the scope of our competitive and odd sisterhood. There were moments when we were friends, parents, rivals, and allies all rolled into one. It seemed that there was a time and a place for everything.

the party and instructed, "Photo on three. One. Two. Three."

He clicked the button just as Stacy returned the favor and pinched the back of my armpit through the velvet material of my dress. I jolted like a maniac. Instead of retaliating with an even larger pinch, I sighed and decided it was karma for my earlier behavior.

Stacy giggled, "Why didn't you just tell us to say cheese, Evan?"

He held out his hand and returned the camera to me. Evan explained, "It feels too demanding. I don't want to tell people to smile if that's not what they're feeling. Whatever people want to do for a picture is fine with me."

Stacy stood just behind him and mouthed, "Marry him."

I did my best not to roll my eyes. "Yeah, encourage whatever behavior comes to mind. Like pinching the back of my arm."

"I did not do that, Lacy. I didn't pinch you back. I was thinking about it, but I decided not to ruin our

Oddly enough, Stacy did sound sincere. I wanted to believe her, but I knew that someone had pinched my arm and there weren't any other suspects.

I flipped around the new digital camera and looked at our photos together. The first image nearly gave me a heart attack. My fingers grew tense as the color drained from my face.

Evan quickly walked over and asked, "Lacy, what's wrong?"

I felt Stacy's concerned gaze as she looked at the side of my face, but I didn't bother to explain. I simply moved the camera so that they both could see the image.

She mumbled, "I'm sure that we don't look that bad. We barely even had half a glass of wine—"

The rest of the sentence died in the back of her throat as she glanced at the image of our smiling faces. However, a dark ominous figure stood directly behind my back. It looked like a woman in a Victorian era dress. The ghoul hovered right over my shoulder as Stacy and I smiled at the camera, completely oblivious to her presence.

expected there to be some sort of ghostly figure. Instead, motel guests stood around the tables and served themselves more wine and coffee. None of them wore clothes from another century. It was as if the apparition was simply a camera glitch, but something in my gut told me that there was more to this than a simple lighting trick.

Stacy looked around the room, equally as confused and muttered, "Maybe the ghost hunters will get a real story after all."

Motel guests had trickled out of the living room and slowly flowed out to the front yard. The afternoon sunlight had felt unusually warm for the typically frigid December evening.

The rest of Stacy's birthday party had moved in a blur of smiles and champagne clinks. However, my mind constantly crawled back and nagged about the unexplained presence that ominously hovered behind my back in the photo. The dark outline had appeared thick and almost physical. It had remained just intangible enough to look like a thick dark plume of smoke.

Evan had stayed after the celebration and helped to clean up the discarded cups and plates. He had even agreed to come over early the next week to help decorate the motel. Secretly, I wondered how he could possibly have so much free time, especially as the owner of his own business. Maybe running a business was easier once it wasn't just one bad mistake away from imploding. The idea of financial stability held its own sort of appeal.

Stacy swore that Evan had willingly stayed to clean up because he liked me. The idea was nice, but I interests.

***

Christmas was always a big deal in our small and sleepy town. It only made sense that that we had decided to buy a little more into the commercialized holiday cheer this year. Stacy had bought more tree ornaments and even purchased a garland wrapped around the long and winding stair banister. The old tree ornaments were a bit of a wash. They were all neon pink, courtesy of the 80's and didn't exactly flow with the Victorian style of the house. We compromised, and Stacy had agreed to use the neon pink ornaments strictly on the miniature tree in her bedroom. Speaking of trees, I needed to pull the Christmas tree out from the creepy basement.

There were less than a handful of days left before the television crew was supposed to arrive. The show had said that they planned to arrive the weekend before Christmas; it was just in time for them to see the old home in all of its former festive glory.

Stacy and I had just finished dragging out the minimum decorations for the holiday season. My cheeks

159

nowhere to be found. After the birthday party debacle, I couldn't think of anywhere else in the world that sounded worse than the basement. The single lightbulb swayed in a circular motion as I flicked it on and descended the creaky wooden steps. Each little squeak threatened to send me sprinting back up the stairs. We could always buy a real tree; forget the budget. Besides, that would definitely add to the authenticity of the entire holiday.

I nervously glanced around the dark basement and noticed several piles of discarded moving boxes. Where had we placed that silly tree? I couldn't remember the last time that we had actually used it in the motel. My bet was on several years ago.

Without even noticing it, we had turned the motel into a regular holiday Scrooge. Well, there was no time like the present to start believing in a little holiday magic.

I mumbled, "Have a little faith, Lacy. You will find this fake tree before next Christmas. Now, where did we put it?"

steps above me.

Startled, I nearly slipped down the last few wooden slats. Luckily, a firm arm wrapped around my upper bicep and kept me from tumbling into the land of hidden spiders and long-forgotten Barbie dolls.

Rattled, I roughly patted Evan's shoulder and hissed, "When did you get here?"

"Just a few minutes ago. Stacy said that you could use some help in the basement with the tree."

I contemplated his explanation and decided that it was more than fair. It wasn't his fault that my own ghostly lies had turned me into a jumpy person. Well, that and the actual possibility of living in a haunted motel.

"Thanks. For the record, you seem to pop up more than the supposed spirits."

"It's a skill. After you live with three older sisters, you learn how to tactfully go unnoticed."

"I didn't know that you had three older siblings."

Evan shrugged as he reached the bottom of the basement, "You never asked."

161

Christmas items. I licked my lower lip and said, "Tell me about them."

There was a moment of silence as Evan looked off into the distance. He stood between a memory and reality, and there I was, patiently waiting for him to bridge the gap and return to the present.

Evan's gaze slowly turned back to my petite form as his stare shifted between me and something in the past that I couldn't even begin to imagine; that was his secret and his alone. Part of me felt like I could wiggle the information out of him, but a larger part of me felt like that just wouldn't be right. Whatever he wanted to volunteer when down in this basement was more than fine. It wasn't like I deserved an award for being the most open and honest person.

The small lightbulb flickered and swung around the room with the help of a steady breeze that I knew was there, but I still couldn't see. The hairs on the back of my arms slowly stood to attention. I glanced around the room and decided that such an ancient building was logically bound to have a sizable draft. Sure, that sounded like a perfectly valid explanation.

box onto his shoulder. It looked somewhat small in size instead of completely unreasonable and impossibly heavy. The box had hardly budged when I had tried to shove it.

I challenged, "What am I doing?"

Evan chuckled, "You're thinking about what's creeping around this house in the middle of the night. You get a strange look on your face when you're worried and this motel could be haunted."

"I didn't know that. I'll be sure to fix that before we ever play poker."

"Deal. Hold the door."

I took two creaky stairs at a time. I was just about to hold the basement door open when it suddenly slammed shut. A gust of wind whirled through the air as the door closed mere inches away from the tip of my nose.

A zing of trepidation scampered down my spine as I instinctively rushed to the door. Maybe Evan was confused on how it opened. Panicked, I wiggled the door handle and when that didn't work, I pounded on the door.

163

wood was so flimsy and old that it often felt similar to a thick piece of paper. I pushed harder and soon realized that it felt even stronger than before; this wasn't possible.

Nervous, I took a step back and then pounded against the door with the side of my shoulder. Searing pain rippled up my arm.

I moaned in dismay; it felt as if the door had been made from stone. I barely registered the gentle shuffle from behind me as Evan likely lowered the massive Christmas box to the ground.

After a few seconds, he squeezed around me and tried to shove open the door with a firm press. The door acted as if nothing had happened. Evan mumbled, "That's an impressive door."

I muttered, "Usually, it's anything but impressive. It's over a century old and probably full of mildew."

Evan joked, "Do you think that we caught it on a bad day?"

in the basement at a more convenient time."

Evan's humor managed to quell my usually high-strung demeanor. It was a horrible time to be inconvenienced right before the film crew arrived, but somehow Evan made it seem like an adventure. His fresh positive perspective was an extremely welcomed take on a ghoulish nightmare.

My eyes wandered around the poorly lit room as I desperately hoped to find a tool that would lead to our release. Maybe a previous motel owner had left a spare crowbar somewhere or even an extremely outdated toolbox.

Motivated, I crept down the stairs as Evan continued to pound against the door. Something told me that the door would eventually open, but it just wouldn't have anything to do with our efforts. It apparently had a mind of its own, just like the living room window earlier last week.

Suddenly, a faint glimmer managed to pull my gaze away from the stubborn door. A tiny key caught my attention, and then I bent down to retrieve the metallic object. It rested in the center of my palm and was barely objects were actually designed to last.

I furtively glanced in Evan's direction and relaxed once I noticed that he was still too preoccupied with the door to even notice the odd shine. I then stealthily slipped the key within the confines of my bra.

Casually, I returned to my half-hearted search for a toolbox. I doubted that such an item would be anywhere visible or convenient. However, almost as soon as I walked away with the mysterious key, the basement door swung open. The abrupt motion looked similar to an automated door in the grocery stores. The odd detail sent the tiny hairs on the back of my neck into a tizzy. I knew for a fact that the door only opened inward, but somehow, it had managed to ignore its own hinges. My heart felt like it was going into overdrive.

Less than a second after the door swung open, Stacy quickly came into view. She placed her hands on her slim hips and sighed, "There you are! I've been looking for both of you for twenty minutes. What do you want for lunch? We need a little break before we keep going."

were both at a loss for words. Eventually, Evan ran a hand through his tousled hair and replied, "Whatever you want to make sounds delicious. I'm starved."

Stacy gave me a questioning look. From my position, several feet lower on the basement stairs, Stacy almost felt like an adult scolding two kids — almost. It was obvious from her poorly contained state that she assumed something more than just moving Christmas decorations had happened between Evan and me in the basement.

In a way, she wasn't wrong. Something different and supernatural had happened, but something told me that that wasn't what Stacy had had in mind. Not that I had any plans to correct her. I had no plans or interest in trying to explain or understand the possible ghost activities.

Instead, I quickly brushed against Evan's shoulder and took the steps two at a time in order to escape from the basement. I said, "We couldn't find the Christmas decorations, so we will need to go to the store to get some more supplies."

untruth. The contact sent a flurry of butterflies whirling around my belly, but kept up my best poker face.

The poker face wasn't working — plan B.

Instead, I placed my weight on the top of Evan's shoes and slyly stepped on his foot. Not that it seemed to matter to him as a pleased smirk crossed his handsome features.

Stacy missed the look as she distractedly glanced at the kitchen and tossed out, "That's fine. The decorations were all from the eighties anyway. I'm not sure what would have been salvageable unless we wanted to make this year's Christmas theme the miracle of tacky and indestructible garlands."

Evan chuckled as he firmly shut the door to the basement. He jiggled the handle for good measure and the entire door managed to rattle with his casual touch. The wood looked as though it was one good shove away from splintering in half.

I cautioned, "Careful, Mr. Smooth. That door is one tiny shove from breaking. I wouldn't really care, but we still need to commit to making this motel spooky

Evan simply nodded and watched as Stacy headed into the kitchen. Once Stacy was out of earshot, I tilted my head to the side and sent Evan a questioning look. Obviously, we had experienced the exact same strange event, but I couldn't find the right words to express the anomaly.

Instead, I sighed, "Maybe we won't need to try so hard to convince the people from the television show that this place is haunted."

Evan chuckled as he casually shoved a hand in his pocket and asked, "I thought you didn't believe in ghosts."

"I don't, but I'm struggling to find feasible answers. I'm not saying that there is a perfectly logical explanation. I'm just saying that at first glance, it seems a little difficult to ignore the basics of the evidence." I folded my arms over my chest; the action pressed the smooth metal of the key closer to my heart and I wondered exactly what it could open.

My mind drifted to the locked box still left inside of my bedroom. It seemed like a completely farfetched option, but stranger things had happened.

unlock the secrets of the motel. Unfortunately, that wasn't as simple as I had planned.

"Hello, Lacy. Back so soon. I must say that you're making a habit of coming to the library."

"Good morning, Mrs. Smith. I just wanted to see a little more of the newspaper records. I'm hoping that at least something in there will help clear up a few of my questions."

Mrs. Smith smiled and waved her arm in the general direction of the basement. Her thin papery skin seemed nearly translucent in the early morning light.

It was so early that all of the desks were empty of curious browsing students and elderly grandparents using the communal computers. That crowd tended to arrive closer to four in the afternoon. Instead, it was just Mrs. Smith, and the longer that I looked at her, the bigger a question formed in the back of my mind.

I wondered just how much Mrs. Smith knew about the history behind the motel. The older woman might have had some useful information from her decades of living in our quiet town. Maybe she had more than one piece of information that I had failed to collect.

to know anything about the mystery behind the motel? Do you know anything about the previous owners before my parents?"

Mrs. Smith's thin pale eyebrows momentarily shot above the thick brim of her glasses at the offhanded question. She placed a spindly hand on her hip and hummed deep in thought. Her eyes narrowed to small perceptive daggers as she looked back into memories from the past.

Eventually, Mrs. Smith made a popping sound with her lips as she began, "From what I know, the old home used to have a somewhat spooky reputation. As a kid, we used to claim that the place on the very top of the hill was haunted. Apparently, something had happened up there to a woman who had disappeared well before I was born. The legend somehow lived on for years until it was eventually forgotten. I can't really remember the full story, but I can remember a few bits and pieces whispered about on the playground. The woman had had a tense relationship with her father and had ended up disappearing right before her wedding. It had been the talk of the town. Did that help?"

that Mrs. Smith had told me with the newspaper clippings. The two stories seemed so similar, but still felt extremely disjointed at the same time. The newspaper had crafted a picture of a doting father that loved his only daughter. *Why was that not the story that Mrs. Smith had heard?*

"Thank you, Mrs. Smith. That's very helpful. If you remember anything else, please let me know."

Mrs. Smith handed me the key to the downstairs records and winked, "Have fun, Dearie."

I tentatively walked down the stairs and headed into the cold basement. I half-heartedly greeted, "So we meet again."

An hour later, I felt like giving up. There was no way to claim that anything strange had truly happened in the motel. In fact, it mostly sounded like an unanswered mystery that could likely just be due to a family scandal. I reasoned that the woman could have been falsely reported missing and sent out of town to avoid a possible scandal.

"That's about as far as I go."

jumped, and the dull thud of my return to Earth resounded around the empty room. I looked around in every direction and quickly realized that there wasn't another soul around.

My fingers shakily reached out and grabbed the projector slides. Something in my belly told me that it was important. I pulled out the projector and swiftly plugged the ancient machine into an outlet.

I then placed the slide into the projector and swiftly enhanced the quality of the image. My feet crept closer to the screen as my eyes quickly widened in surprise. The newspaper article dated back a year before the unknown woman had supposedly disappeared.

An image remained on the very front of the newspaper of a young woman as she looked into the distance directly in front of the motel. I read the headline and quickly recognized her last name.

"Lockwood."

I guessed that the woman was either the wife or daughter of the original owner of the motel. However, something in the woman's demeanor made me guess that she was in fact a steadfast and strong-willed daughter.

many photographs often depicted a life that was so much harder than today. The traces of a smile were barely discernible on her dainty features. The article's title managed to raise even more questions as it mentioned how the young woman had apparently saved the library from ruin by hosting a barn-raising event in its honor.

I remembered learning about those in school. It had been common for neighbors to come together and celebrate the raising of a barn or a building as a community. It was clear that this young woman had both social pull and a healthy amount of gumption to arrange such a massive undertaking in a part of the country where both tools and people were often scarce. It was even more impressive because the entire town had apparently been so dedicated to the idea of a library that they had eagerly come together on a Saturday to complete the task.

Curious, I wondered what the old library had looked like and if the woman from the photograph had ever walked on the same exact spot as me. The question sent a shiver down my spine; the strong reaction made

The article left me with more questions than answers. I wondered how it was possible for a woman so obviously beloved by the community to turn into a missing and possibly dishonorable woman in less than a year.

I groaned, "I'm still missing something."

One more Yahoo search, that's all that I wanted before the camera crew arrived. Well, one more very long perusal of the internet in combination with several helpings of courage.

It was the weekend before Christmas and time had passed in a blur from when the crew had first announced their initial arrival to this morning. It felt like a dream and I still wasn't sure if it was a dream come true or the calm before the storm in a perilous nightmare.

Thanks to Evan, the motel looked brighter than usual with a fresh layer of paint and spotless new carpet in the living room. He had called it an early Christmas present, and it was honestly the most romantic gesture I'd ever received. Every time that I walked into living room, I thought about him and his kind gentle eyes. He was definitely a romantic genius in my mind.

A goofy smile crept along the edges of my lips as I thought about Evan more than I wanted to admit. He had brought more than just a clean new perspective to the living room.

story just kept getting stranger, even though the clues available within the library had long run dry. I couldn't help feeling like there was a massive piece of the puzzle that was still missing.

At around three in the morning, Evan had left earlier the motel with dark circles underneath his eyes, but an excited bounce in his step. Luckily, he didn't work at the garage on Saturdays, so he had promised to come over to meet the television crew after a well-earned cat nap. Honestly, it had surprised me that he was so committed to helping even though we had grown nearly inseparable in less than three months. The speed of our friendship scared me, but I actively avoided overthinking it.

In three short months, it now felt odd not to say goodnight to him or to hear him call in the morning just so that he could hear all about the antics that the motel guests tended to get into during the middle of the night. Apparently, most of the guests were convinced that the ghosts and spirits were only active during the night. Several brave guests had wandered into the basement and attic without the slightest concern for their own

Personally, I felt that the only thing that was active were their wild imaginations. Spirits and ghosts weren't real.

I had decided that what Evan and I had witnessed a few weeks ago in the basement was simply a stress-induced groupthink brain fart. Of course, the door wouldn't open. We had been too panicked to function let alone use our motor skills and brains.

"A ton of vans are coming down the driveway!" Stacy burst into my bedroom and the door bounced against the wall.

My eyebrow arched in disapproval as I slowly stood from my tiny desk that had quickly become the epicenter of the paranormal television debacle.

Stacy wore a pair of dark flare jeans and a sensible knit top; she looked professional and presentable in a way that made me wish our parents could see.

We had both decided to dress tastefully to meet the crew. However, we weren't afraid to dress like people from the 1800s to greet them if the situation turned desperate. We were more than willing to put aside was one more desperate grab for attention?

A deep sigh escaped into the room as I walked over and grabbed Stacy's hand. It slightly trembled just like my own did with a mix of trepidation and a sliver of excitement.

"Are you ready?" I waited for her response.

Even though she was taller than me, Stacy was still my younger sister. We were in this mess together, but I still wanted to make ensure that she was okay; it was an ironic emotion considering that my tipsy choices had dragged her into this mess.

Unsurprisingly, she put on the biggest grin and eagerly nodded her head in agreement. She shrugged her shoulders and added, "There is no time like the present."

"Thank you for doing this, Stacy. You know, it's not too late. You and Jeffrey can leave and pretend not to be available this weekend. It would probably be better for both of you." My eyes squinted at a spot of slightly clumpy new white paint that was just above Stacy's head.

Stacy squeezed my hand with gentle pressure as she laughed, "This is the biggest adventure of my life.

"You hate group projects, Stacy."

"Not this one."

I paused as a ball of emotion steadily built within the back of my throat. Some words felt stuck on the tip of my tongue and really needed to be said. Stacy noticed my struggle and waited for me.

Finally, I managed, "You know that mom and dad would be very proud of you, right? You are so sweet and kind. I know that I don't give you enough credit and can really get on your back about the motel, but you really are the best sister in the entire world."

On the spur of the moment, mist appeared in Stacy's bright eyes, and she blinked away the tears that threatened to fall. She then drew in a deep breath through her nose at the mention of our parents. It was a touchy subject since we rarely mentioned them even on birthdays. It was really just too hard to relive all of those memories. However, it really did feel like the situation called for a certain amount of naked honesty— a rare moment of truth that forced only the rawest emotions to the surface.

181

answer. You are just as welcome to go to Jeffrey's place for the weekend. I can give you a full report about what happens on Monday."

Stacy paused for a moment as she shifted her weight from one slender hip to the other. Then she tilted her head to the side and playfully narrowed her eyes, "I know that, but that would be no fun. It's the biggest adventure in the history of this motel. You're my big sister and you always do everything to keep me safe. I'm not so little anymore. I can do just fine on my own, but you're always there and always worrying. One tiny interesting life choice isn't going to change that love. Who knows? Maybe the camera crew will be a good thing? Nothing is really ever certain until it's finished and even then, who is to say when something is really ever done? Mom and dad died, but we still love them and think about them. That love is still in this motel so maybe in some ways it is haunted because something outside of our understanding does live inside of these walls. Look, what I'm trying to say is that we are doing this together. No matter what happens."

She then crooked the edges of her lips up into a smile and asked, "Oh, and Lacy?"

"Yeah?"

"Mom and dad are also proud of you, too. They're always with us, even if we can't see that from here. Just because we can't see the full image doesn't mean that other parts of it don't exist. We just have to trust that there is more than what we can see."

"Did you read that in one of those new age books? Because that's honestly really beautiful, Stacy."

Stacy laughed and the noise gently filled the hallway as she added, "No. It was something that one of the older ladies told me at church before I stopped going. I guess it stuck with me."

"Never gone."

"Never."

A sharp ring emanated from downstairs, and it was evident that the crew was finally ready to be let in. I shook out my shoulders and gripped Stacy's hand just a little tighter.

She instantly returned the gesture as we said everything we needed to say to each other with one final the details of those memories, but the exact feeling effortlessly returned as though it had never left.

Stacy wiggled her nose and waited for me to say it was time. We were in the eye of the storm and it felt calm and isolated from the reality that rang the doorbell downstairs.

I gave her a small smile, "Let's go."

We walked down the unusually bright hallway that suddenly seemed enormous, then turned the corner and headed down the stairs with our hands interlocked.

The temperamental front door opened so easily for the camera crew that I was partially convinced that it was floating on its hinges. It was the first time that the door hadn't felt unreasonably heavy, but part of me decided that it was just my own nerves playing a trick on me.

A round petite woman stood on the other side of the door. Large glasses hid most of her face and emphasized her large doe-like green eyes. She looked like a sweet elderly woman that was prepared for an afternoon adventure in the park. Instead, it was obvious that she was leading the ghost hunting expedition.

She chimed, "Hello! You must be the owners of The Mistletoe Motel. It's so nice to finally meet both of you in person. Can we come in and start setting up?"

A small apprehensive smile crept along the edges of my lips as I held out my hand and greeted, "Welcome to the motel. This is my sister Stacy and my name is Lacy."

"My name is Magda. We spoke earlier on the phone. Your parents must really love a good rhyme."

living room. A strong gust of air whirled into the room from the entrance and whipped around my freshly curled hair. The weather had previously been calm and manageable, but now it seemed to pick up energy.

Magda's green eyes widened in embarrassment as her plump cheeks turned a more flushed shade of red. She dipped her head down as she added, "My apologies."

I felt bad for conveying such personal information so flippantly. Luckily, I managed to save the mood as I reassured, "Don't worry. We like to think that people have a way of lingering after they go."

Magda quickly nodded her head in agreement as she reached out and cupped both of my hands. She clutched a clip board under her arm as she gingerly squeezed my palms. Magda swiftly agreed, "You're right. That's partly why I decided to produce this show. It's a very interesting concept to believe and understand that there is more to life than what we can see. I am excited to look around your lovely motel with the rest of the Scare Squad. Now, it's important not to get your hopes up about your motel being haunted. It's very it's just a few drafty hallways or an overly zealous host that tends to loosen floor boards and hinges in order to scare the easily spooked guests."

Stacy guffawed, "Can you believe that, Lacy? Loosened hinges?"

Instead of making eye contact, I kept my eyes trained on the activity happening around the room. I wasn't sure if my poor poker face would effectively hide my shame.

I knew what Stacy meant as she hinted at the questionable hinges on the basement door. The momentary break in the conversation was a welcomed respite.

It had been years since a stranger had accidentally stepped into the topic of our dead parents. Of course, it wasn't like Stacy or I gave many people the chance. We rarely left the motel. Most of the people that we usually spoke to were already old friends of our family like Letty.

It felt strange to even vaguely mention mom and dad with a stranger that had the potential power to ruin the motel, but the realization certainly held a twinge of items in the furthest corner near the fireplace. My body felt firmly planted on the new carpet, but my mind felt as if it was drifting a million miles away.

Magda narrowed her eyes and glanced back at her crew. She had a sparkle in her eyes that seemed to hint at her excitement. She turned to one of the men holding a massive camera case and instructed, "Please open that case, Mitchell. It's likely that we've already been detected by a possible entity."

I glanced over at Stacy and noticed that she had bit down on her lower lip. It was obvious that she was struggling to maintain her composure.

Stacy and I both knew that it was critical that we took the show seriously. Even if we both felt like there was absolutely no way that the motel was haunted. We needed to at least act like it was worth the benefit of the doubt.

Mitchell walked over and wiped his sweaty palms on his pants as his eyes shone with excitement. It looked like he was struggling to keep his eagerness under control.

direction of the case and asked, "What's in there?"

The stout man named Mitchell glanced at Magda and asked for confirmation before he explained, "These are just some of the tools that we plan to use in order to find potential ghosts. There is more than just one way to find the truth. Don't worry, we are also doing more traditional methods, too. We hired a medium in order to try and speak to the spirits. She should be here around seven in the evening. We like to think that paranormal activity really gains strength during the night."

I was momentarily at a loss for words. Instead, I nodded my head and agreed, "That sounds exciting."

"Should we put the lights in here?" A man in a black shirt called from across the room at a volume that sounded as if he was actually trying to raise the dead.

Pun intended.

Magda squinted her eyes at the lights and then waved an arm across her chest, "No. Put the camera and lights in that corner. We should face the wall and record away from the windows. Windows can bring in a distracting glare and viewers always think that there is something outside."

Stacy leaned down so that her face was level with my ear as she whispered, "Isn't that the point? To make it seem like there are strange things happening from beyond?"

I leaned to the right and lightly stepped on her foot in warning. The last thing that we needed was to be overheard making fun of their profession. There was no reason to stir the pot anymore than needed.

Suddenly, the doorbell rang. I excused myself from the room and headed over to see if we had any potential guests. We had agreed to leave the hotel at half

However, that private agreement wasn't common knowledge for the curious traveler.

I opened the door and my jaw nearly hit the floor in disbelief. No way.

"Take it off, Evan."

A deep chuckle resonated from the back of his throat as he winked at me as if everything was fine. He asked, "You don't like my new look?"

"You look like my great-great grandfather that fought in the Civil War."

"Was he North or South?"

"North."

"Sounds about right. Is it the hair, Lacy? The wig really adds some personality."

I swatted at his chest as I fully absorbed the absurdity of his outfit. Even though I was slightly disgruntled, a much larger part of my heart felt strangely elated. No one would even bat an eye at me with Evan by my side. An invisible weight lifted from my shoulders. He looked absolutely ridiculous.

front door.

He took several steps closer and his mint scented breath fanned against the heated skin of my face as he goaded, "I know, but that's what makes me so interesting."

"That and your fashion sense."

"You know that you need to be careful, Lacy."

I tilted my head to the side, "Why?"

"In this outfit, I might just become a catch to any young ghost within a twenty mile radius."

I rolled my eyes and quipped, "I don't think that people in the late 1800s wore powdered wigs. I'm pretty sure that was more from the 1700s. It's still a very nice touch."

"Thanks for the compliment, Lacy." He playfully wiggled his thick eyebrows and then stepped back a few paces.

The added space gave me a moment to defog my momentarily clouded mind. I cleared my throat and hesitantly looked at him.

Just do it, Lacy. I wanted to tell Evan how much I appreciated his antics. He really was going out of his

Instead, I reached out and squeezed his palm. After the brief contact, I quickly returned back to my previous spot.

My anxious fingers played with the old key that I had found at the bottom of the motel basement. It was now indefinitely strung around my neck on a thin gold chain. It hadn't fit into the box that I had discovered in the library, but something still told me to keep the ancient key close, just in case.

"Are you ready?"

"For what?"

"To introduce me to the camera crew."

A laugh bubbled out from the back of my throat. "Absolutely. You should be the first person that they interview."

I had been kidding about the interview. Apparently, the crew and Magda had loved the idea about talking with someone in costume.

Evan patiently waited as a member of the crew applied a light layer of foundation to his face. He sat in the middle of the sofa as his long legs stretched to the side. A small smile played on the edges of my lips at the sight.

He looked over and sent me a playful wink as he was instructed to blot his slightly pink stained lips with a tissue. Evan took it all in stride as the lights turned on and a sound specialist attached a microphone to the top of his elaborate shirt.

Magda grumbled unintelligible words that sounded somewhere between disdain and distaste as she looked at Evan's hulking position in the middle of the fabric sofa. Even in a ridiculous outfit, he looked somewhat imposing thanks to his strong build.

I glanced at Magda as she stifled a curse under her breath before she added, "Bring him a chair. The

A few members of the crew scrambled around the room. Instinctively, I moved into a corner and tried to stay out of the way. This interview was definitely something that needed to be observed from a safe distance.

Magda turned back to Evan once he was seated in a chair and clapped her hands together. She walked over and explained, "Okay, we are just going to ask you a few questions about the motel. If you can tell us anything about the old history then that's even better. We will edit out the questions so it will be just like you are talking and explaining information to the camera."

She then quickly turned to me and then continued, "We will also interview you and Stacy to get the full perspective of the owners. We found that it always works best if we have an opinion from a visitor or town member vouch for the reputation of the potentially haunted location. It tends to bring more life to an episode. Sounds good?"

"Yep, sounds great." I rested my back against the wall and prepared to watch Evan's interview. I hadn't

Magda plucked her trusty clipboard up from its precarious position on the top of a crate and then walked around to the side of a massive video camera. She pointed at the camera and gestured with her hands. She then pointed at Evan and instructed, "Please tell us when you first heard of the motel."

Evan glanced at me from the corner of his eyes before he took in a deep inhale. He widened his shoulders and explained, "I first heard of the motel when I was just a kid. Most everyone in town knew about the Pondwaters. They were the family on the top of the hill that worked around the clock and always made sure that guests left with a smile on their faces. I grew up in the town and had always imagined what it would be like to live here on the top of the hill. I had always wondered what it would feel like to be able to see trees and greenery for miles on end. Of course, there was always the occasional ghost story, but I had never put too much weight into old playground rhymes."

I frowned a little at Evan's words. He didn't need to lie in order to make the crew find the motel more interesting. We were already in enough trouble as it was.

Magda nodded her head in approval as she added, "That's great, Evan. Just try to keep your eyes on the camera. You can't keep looking over at Lacy. I'm sure she won't get mad about anything that you say. Right, Lacy?"

Magda looked over at me with a calm and expectant gaze. Her observant nature momentarily caught me off-guard.

I coughed into the back of my hand and agreed, "Right. Say what you feel like sharing, Evan."

Evan didn't look back at me, but simply nodded his head. His fingers tightly gripped the corner of his pants before he released the fabric and gently placed the palm of his hand back on his knee. The motion seemed so odd since between the two of us, Evan tended to have a much calmer nature. I noticed that the heat of the lamps had also tinted the skin of cheeks a pale pink. The additional camera lights were most definitely hot.

Magda held up the clipboard and buried her face into the content. She hummed in the back of her throat for a minute before she eventually nodded in approval about something that no one else in the room knew

Simple enough.

Evan chuckled, "That's easy. Going up the driveway just a few minutes ago."

"What?" The question left my lips before I even knew that I had thought about it.

Magda wrinkled her nose at me, but I was too absorbed in Evan's response to care. He simply shrugged his shoulders and explained, "I was going around the bend in the curve when suddenly a woman came out of thin air. I thought it was a guest, but by the time I parked and looked around, the figure had already disappeared. She was wearing an odd hat and baggy men's clothing, but she was most definitely a woman."

"Maybe it was just a person from out of town?"

Evan chuckled, "Definitely not. People from out of town rarely leave First Street. The nearest railroad is three miles from here and people rarely go out into the cold without proper snow shoes. Especially during December. They'd never make it more than a mile in this weather. Besides, something about the entire experience just felt unexplainable. It left the hairs on the back of my neck standing up."

voice turned almost imploring as he finished his explanation.

I felt like I could almost see the woman in the back of my mind. A woman that perhaps never really left the woods. However, the story did seem extremely convenient. What were the odds that Evan would see the first real ghost on the property? All we had experienced so far were a few odd creaks and a scary basement door. The door in question, I had just replaced the lock right before the film crew came to visit. The last thing that I wanted was a repeat of such a heart pounding experience. I wasn't sure if I would be able to stay stuck down there all alone. It was just too spooky, even if it wasn't actually haunted.

Magda nudged, "I see. When was the second most recent supernatural encounter that you've had? Perhaps something that's actually inside of the motel?"

A goofy smile crept across Evan's face as he added, "I was with Lacy. We had ended up trapped in the basement. The door had become stuck, but the wood is pretty old so in reality I should have been able to break it down. In the moment, it had felt like a steel door that

Magda added, "What were you two doing down in the basement?"

Evan nodded his head in understanding and elaborated, "We had headed into the basement to find the old Christmas decorations. Instead, the door had slammed shut with an unexpected breeze or something. More accurately, it was like some invisible hand had closed the door. The door to the basement is in the middle of the downstairs so there aren't any windows around and it's very unlikely that we had left any windows open seeing as it had been a relatively cold day. We were pretty nervous until the door seemed to open on its own. It was as if nothing had happened. After that, we had decided to just go into town and buy the rest of the decorations. We didn't see the point in testing fate for a second time."

Magda said, "Thank you Evan." Her eyes skimmed a piece of paper until she landed on a question near the bottom. Her eyes crinkled near the corners in a look close to excitement as she asked, "Do you personally believe in ghosts?"

moment to collect his thoughts before he responded, "I don't know. Maybe it's all a collective trick of the imagination, but it felt pretty real to me. I would like to think that we all end up somewhere after we die. Our memory at least lives on in the people that we met during our lives. Maybe ghosts and supernatural experiences happen because we lend power to the idea. Maybe we die and that's it. Maybe if you're good then you end up seeing the pearly gates. It's not really like there is much proof on the subject seeing as were all here instead of on the other side."

Suddenly, all of the windows started to rattle and Evan quickly halted his explanation. It was as though the entire room had grown infuriated with his words. The glass wavered and rippled as the entire wall of windows shook in fury. Each window flew open as a furious breeze whirled into the room.

I released a startled yelp as the cold air harshly bit down against my exposed flesh. In a matter of seconds, Evan stood from his seated position and wrapped a secure hand around my waist. We stood huddled together against the corner of the wall.

gripped the side of Evan's shirt.

Within seconds, the wind disappeared. The windows swung on their hinges until they suddenly stopped all movement. There was no warning or slowing of movement. Just an instantaneous halt. It was as if nothing had even happened.

My jaw dropped open as I surveyed the mess. Papers were strewn about the room and people huddled together at the corners furthest away from the windows.

Magda carefully walked into the center of the room and propped her clipboard onto her hip. She slowly spun around in a circle and then asked, "Right. Did anyone get that on camera?"

Unsurprisingly, the crew had decided to take a break after the window debacle. Magda flitted around the downstairs and took notes about possible areas that she could use as backgrounds for the rest of the interviews. The majority of the crew seemed less than enthused. A few of them darted nervous glances at the windows as if they would burst open at any moment and allow the small smattering of raindrops to enter the motel.

I walked into the kitchen and allowed Magda her much needed time to explore. It didn't really matter since I had placed all of our valuables inside of our locked truck. Just in case. Jeffrey had simply shrugged his shoulders and then handed me his wallet and three different varieties of sage that no doubt belonged to my sister. Fair enough.

"That was some interview, Evan." Jeffrey chopped a few carrots after Stacy washed them clean.

It was almost five in the evening and we had decided to prepare dinner for the television crew before the night activities commenced. The last thing that we

Evan laughed as he stirred a pot that was filled to the brim with tomato soup. It smelled delicious.

"Can I help?"

The question was met by Stacy's loud laugh as she wiped a fake tear from the corner of her eye. She looked between Evan and then glanced back at me. It seemed like she had decided that it was better not to make another comment about my obviously lacking culinary talent.

Unfortunately, Evan had already picked up on her obvious reaction as he slowed his stirring and asked, "What do you mean? Lacy, do you struggle with cooking?"

There it was, the dreaded question. It wasn't that I didn't want to learn, but it was more so the fact that cooking tended to take time and usually I was absolutely exhausted once I finally remembered to eat.

"I am more of a Veggiefresh Promise pizza kind of gal. Not by pure disinterest, but by sheer lack of skill." My hands subconsciously waved away several invisible stray strands of hair.

walked over and sat down on a bar stool near the kitchen island as Stacy started working with the boxes of shell-shaped noodles.

He patted the table and explained, "Lacy is always amazing around the motel. She's figured out how to stretch the dollars and repurpose old roof shingles on more than one occasion. It's one of her very best skills. Cooking is one of her most dangerous attributes, but that's what keeps her humble."

"That's not completely true." I mumbled the words under my breath, but I decided not to add kindling to my own roast.

Evan squinted his eyes as a bead of sweat rolled down the side of his ridiculous wig. His costume looked extremely warm as he continued to work over the flaming hot industrial sized stove.

I called, "You know that you can take the wig off now."

Evan tutted, "No way. I'm not breaking character. That's acting 101. No changing the subject. What kind of example can you provide that proves that

Stacy easily jumped in and explained, "She managed to melt a spatula into a pan. That just happened last week."

Red tinted my cheeks when I recalled the recent memory. It wasn't exactly my finest moment, but the spatula had been promptly replaced by a sturdy wooden one that was much less likely to turn into mush.

"It's okay, Lacy. Everyone has something that they just can't wrangle. Mine is a deep fear of moths and the dark."

"Moths?"

"They have wings and they can't be trusted." He gave the pot a final inspection and then accepted the freshly cut vegetables from Stacy's outstretched hand.

"Thank you."

The room erupted into laughter and for once an easy peace entered the motel. It felt so nice to have a moment of warmth shared between family and friends. A lightness seemed to lift the weight from my shoulders that I hadn't even known was present. It was like running a marathon on a sprained ankle and only

The door to the kitchen swung open and Magda's face practically glowed as she chimed, "We have placed cameras in most of the rooms. We are ready to start as soon as the medium arrives."

Jeffrey ladled the piping hot soup into bowls as Stacy carefully placed them on the counter. He asked, "Should we make one for the medium?"

Magda's nose wrinkled. After less than a day of knowing her, the motion seemed to mean that the answer was something along the lines of no. I couldn't tell if her wrinkled nose also meant that she found a certain comment relatively upsetting, but I had a hunch that was also included.

The older woman simply shook her head as she struggled to explain, "Our medium has a very precise way of doing things. Don't provide her with any additional information if she asks you a question and don't offer her any food that has been prepared inside of the motel. She likely will have already eaten something before she arrives."

Magda then nodded her head and hastened, "But thank you so much for feeding all of the crew members happily join you for dinner. Thank you."

Jeffrey humbly nodded his head and added, "It was a group effort."

I hopped into the conversation with a little well-intended self-deprecation and added, "Not really. Some of us were encouraged not to help."

Evan walked over and placed the palm of his hand over my shoulder and lightly squeezed as he teased, "I was told that it was for the best."

"Safety first."

"Absolutely, Lacy."

Magda silently stood near the kitchen door, not exactly sure how to respond. Her eyes remained wide and full of questions as she turned and glanced at each of us in turn. Eventually, she sucked her lower lip between her teeth as she smiled. Her lips looked thinner than usual in such an odd position. Finally, she released them and added, "Thanks, again for dinner."

"It will be ready in about five minutes." Jeffrey instructed as he was nearly half-way finished with filling the bowls.

enough for that task so I quickly filled a pitcher with water and headed over to the long table.

However, an odd blur of movement halted me in my steps. I watched completely transfixed as the elaborate skirt of a dress slowly ghosted around the bend in the hallway. The movement happened so fast that the colors and details seemed blurred just to the point that the sight felt hazy.

Scattered, I tried to recall if any of the current guests enjoyed wearing long elaborate dresses, but all of them seemed like supernatural enthusiast. However that I couldn't recall guests wearing anything other than jeans or cargo pants. It also didn't hurt that a long skirt was exceptionally impractical given today's cold dreary weather.

I turned the corner at a slow cautious pace. Careful to give whatever had been ahead of me enough time to disappear before I rounded the next corner.

Dinner had ended without anything remarkable happening. The crew members were all very polite and had even offered to help clear the plates. The incident from earlier in the day felt like a distant memory after a helping of hearty soup and fresh warm bread. It wasn't massive, but the meal was enough that there were just about two servings left within the massive pot.

I stretched my arms up to the ceiling and momentarily walked behind the front desk. This all felt like unchartered territory, but my nerves had slightly settled after getting to know the people situated around the dinner table. They felt a little less like obvious strangers and a little more like casual work associates.

Apparently, one of the camera women absolutely loved our small town and even wanted to stay at the motel after filming the episode. She said that she wanted to bring her family and show off what she felt was easily one of the more active locations. It struck me as odd that someone who had obviously traveled to more than a few haunted places had found our little motel so interesting.

My fingers flitted over unused tour itineraries and old maps of the highly frequented hiking trails around town. I wanted to show the camera woman a few more activities that were offered nearby. Selfishly, I really hoped that she'd stay in the motel if she ever decided to visit the town with her family. Personally, I wasn't exactly sure what she was so excited about seeing as we only had a very questionable draft in the living room.

Magda shuffled over with a barely contained bounce in her step as a woman in her late sixties also approached near the desk. The stranger wore a long black dress that was so perfectly fitted that the edges of the material practically ghosted across the surface of the floor. Her white hair shone with an elegant brightness as it reflected against the motel lights. Not a single tendril seemed out of place from her perfectly maintained bun. Her eyes looked slightly hazy as if age had suddenly crept up upon her body and partly claimed her sight. Overall, she looked almost ethereal in nature.

I knew who the woman was before Magda could even introduce her.

Our sentences overlapped at the same time and we both chuckled at our somewhat shared excitement. We looked at each other in a strange combination of amusement and embarrassment.

The woman, given no other title besides medium, eventually interjected, "Shall we begin?"

Her demeanor wasn't exactly friendly, but it was obvious that she was already on the job as her cool eyes flitted around the room and examined every nook and cranny. I was glad that I had actually taken the time to clean the stray cobwebs that had hung near the entrance of the doors. The process hadn't taken long, but it had been relatively cumbersome to reach around the corners on a ladder.

Her near translucent stare returned to my face and quickly pulled me back into the moment. I gave her a small smile and asked, "Would you like me to give you a tour?"

She nodded her head and explained, "Now, it's very important that you remember not to give me unneeded information. Don't lead me with details that could taint my communication with the other side. Try to

I frowned. How did she know that my online summary of the motel was a hoax in such a short amount of time? The hairs on the back of my neck bristled in intense irritation.

"Why would you say that?" The question wrestled free of my vice-like control and I looked down the hall in an effort to shield my features from her eyes that seemed to detect even the smallest hint of insincerity. The flecks of white in her eyes were illuminated by the whites of her irises and the combination produced an unnecessarily eerie image. As the sun slowly set on the horizon, the medium looked more like a celestial being that had somehow mistakenly fallen to Earth.

The woman settled her star-like gaze on something just to the right of my shoulder as she explained, "Because this house is already too noisy. Something tells me that tonight will be an absolute riot."

Her calm voice sent a shiver down my spine. Her cool silky voice stood in stark contrast to her sharp and rigid warning. Her words brokered no arguments about the impending future of the motel.

into a supernatural-related fib. It was possible that this woman had at one point joked about knowing about the paranormal and had quickly ended up too invested in the lie to escape or tell the truth. Maybe she was what I would look like only a few years into the future. It wasn't that far of a stretch.

The medium pivoted on the balls of her feet and turned to exit the kitchen. She called over her shoulder, "We will start with the bedrooms."

"This is my bedroom. I can show you one of the guest rooms that are located on the second floor if you would like. Those rooms have more light since they have better positioned windows." I gripped the locked handle of my bedroom door with a near crippling hold. My fingers turned pale with the amount of pressure that I placed on the door.

"Tell me child, have you ever heard of a partial haunting?" The stars in the medium's aged eyes looked a little bit brighter than before.

I frowned at the odd question and answered, "No."

"Exactly. A spirit doesn't take into account boundaries. A spirit or entity haunts a place however they see fit. I promise that we won't touch or take any of your belongings."

The older woman had a hint of a smile. Her lips were outlined in the thinnest age lines that I had seen.

As if sensing my lingering apprehension, the medium added, "Your bedroom is in the house. Why

She had a point. I pulled out a second key that hung around my neck and quickly unlocked the door handle. The last thing that I wanted was to look more suspicious and unusual than necessary. I pushed the door open and motioned for both Magda and the medium to enter first. So much for privacy.

The medium took a sharp inhale as she looked around the room. She held out a shaky hand and walked around my bed. Her steps grew closer and closer to where I had hidden the mysterious metal box from the library. The medium took two more steps and was practically standing on the box that was positioned only a few inches away and just barely underneath the bed. I was sure that the medium's outstretched hand was exactly above the box as her palm hovered several inches above the bed.

Luckily, Magda coughed from the other corner of the room as she opened my blinds. A small puff of dust whirled into the air and drew the medium's attention.

I felt the skin of my face turn red as I hastily explained, "I don't keep my room to the same standard

216

disorganization in my own space helps me to destress."

I was about to dive into a deeper rambling spiral, but luckily the medium mercifully put me out of my misery. The older woman placed a hand high in the air and motioned for silence.

I drew in my lower lip and bit down as the older woman continued to look around and examine my childhood bedroom. It was such an intimate space to show to a stranger that I almost felt naked. I was very aware of the nicer clothes that were painstakingly arranged to better fit my petite form, but a large part of me still felt completely exposed.

The two women moved around my room and examined every corner. Magda seemed much more interested in moving around and examining the personal contents within the room than the medium. The medium simply stood in the middle of the room and glanced at nothing in particular. It seemed as if her mind was as far away as her constellation speckled eyes.

After a few minutes, the medium slowly looked around and shook her head no. This system seemingly repeated itself on an indefinite loop for the majority of

I opened the other doors and each time, the medium calmly stood near the center of the room as Magda buzzed around like an irritated bumblebee. Magda whirled from one corner to another as a notepad and pen remained clasped as closely to her chest as possible. She looked like an anxious mom on her first day of school. It was obvious from the worried gazes and questionable eyebrow raises that she hadn't expected the medium's indifference.

I felt my heart as it plummeted to my feet. How had I been so naive to think that this plan would work? There were so many people with so many better ideas so why did I think for even a minute that this crazy plan would work?

"Hey, Lacy."

Stacy greeted me from around the corner as her long, usually perfectly brushed mane, looked like it had been through a windstorm. That was unusual. Most of the time, Stacy went out of her way to keep away even the smallest of wayward strands. Her eyes looked wild with excitement. Curious, I mumbled, "What's on your mind?"

I shrugged, "No, but it's the only one that I have."

Magda pursed her lips as the medium went from one room to another with a look of quiet calculated dispassion. The most exciting thing that happened was when the medium had sneezed. Unfortunately, I was pretty sure that the show wasn't looking for invisible and supernatural dust spores.

Uncertainty settled within the pit of my belly as I wondered if everything that I had experienced within the last few weeks had simply been a trick of my own subconscious. Did my mind really conjure up every single odd encounter? I knew that it was completely possible from everything that I had read online. Worse, why was I relying on and clinging onto the glitzy words of a television show psychic to prove my point?

The medium led the way down to the ground floor and wandered the hallway as two cameras silently followed behind. I walked behind the cameras, not exactly sure what to do. The old woman somehow reminded me of a fox on the hunt. I had watched countless old cartoons about hounds on the hunt for

Suddenly, the small older woman stood as straight as a ruler as her shoulders pulled up close to her ears. Her entire body looked so stiff that it almost looked as if she had been struck by lightning.

"What's in here?" The medium's voice turned throaty as one long finger pointed at the newly improved and still closed basement door.

I licked my lower lip and explained, "That's the basement."

"What's down there?"

"Usually, we just store decorations and odd furniture items down there."

After a momentary pause, I decided that there was no time like the present to be transparent about what had happened only a few weeks ago. My voice at first came out as unsure, but slowly gained confidence, "Evan and I ended up stuck down there when we were trying to get the Christmas decorations. The door felt like it was made from solid stone. It didn't make sense because the door at the time had been several decades old and on its last leg. Well, so to speak. Evan is stronger than most people and the door hadn't even budged an inch when he really been down there since the incident because it was just too odd."

The medium listened intently to every detail as her clouded constellation like eyes looked at something in the distance. She seemed to be placing the abstract pieces of the puzzle together in a way that I didn't even want to try.

Once I finished talking, a strange twinkle appeared in the medium's eyes as she asked, "Child, did your parents pass away in this house?"

Discomfort prickled on the top of my skin as if I had just fallen back into the rose bushes that lined the exterior of the motel. I wiggled my shoulders and momentarily glanced at the camera crew as they silently hovered only a few steps away like an unwanted shadow. Bright lights shone on my face and made me feel like I had nowhere to escape. I turned my head slightly to the left and realized that another camera and boom microphone cornered my alternate escape route down the other end of the hallway.

Instantly, the medium made a shooing motion with her hand and the camera crew behind my back all, this was part of the history of the motel. Deep down, I knew that this question would eventually come to the surface.

"Yes. Both our mother and father passed away in this motel. They had spent almost every one of their waking hours trying to turn this place into something special. My dad had actually named it a motel because he had felt that the title of a hotel was too pretentious and the idea of a bed and breakfast just wasn't for them. Growing up, we heard his lengthy explanation almost every year. Every year, we always liked to pretend that it was brand new information, just so that we would be able to have a moment with our dad. He passed away in our parent's bedroom. It's still relatively untouched. It looks more like they decided to go out for a trip one day and just never came back."

"You haven't done anything to move out any items from your parents?"

"Not yet. It really was all just so recent." I ran a hand through my hair and quickly stopped once I remembered how long it had taken Stacy to finally get it into a reasonable state. I mentally cringed as I imagined

The medium nodded her head respectfully and pressed, "How long ago did your parents pass away?"

I responded, "Our mother passed away a little under a decade ago and our father followed about two years ago."

A stale taste crept up the back of my throat as I realized that what had felt like the blink of an eye, had actually been several years. Had we really been in a state of survival with the motel for so many years? How was it possible that time had grown so disconnected from what I viewed as reality?

The frown that crossed my lips was impossible to hide. I didn't bother to hide my displeasure. Instead, I wiped my sweaty palms on the side of my hip and tried to grapple with the possibility that maybe it was time to move forward.

"What was your favorite thing about your parents?"

The question was a welcome reprieve from my suddenly dark train of thought. The frown lines slowly ebbed away as I recalled that one family trip when I had just turned ten. We had all taken a miniature vacation to more time with my family. We were finally away from all of the guests that constantly asked for an extra towel or additional tissue box. It wasn't that I had minded so much about the questions, but I had just wished that there had been more moments with my family spent away from the guests.

However, my father had always said that guests of the motel were just family members that we had yet to formally meet. He had simply insisted that every guest be treated like family because, after all, they were someone else's family.

Always giving.

The memory whirled around in my mind like a load of laundry in the dryer as I explained, "We went on a trip to the lake. The forecast had said that it would be sunny and warm, but as soon as we arrived at the cabin it started pouring rain. I don't think that there had been more than an hour of the clear sky during the entire trip. I loved every second of it. We had played board games together and dad had made all of us hot chocolate as mom had fixed the bunny ears on the television set. It was supposed to be a fun summer weekend, but it had day, my dad had tucked us in for the night and he gave us both such a big hug. It wasn't anything extravagant, but it still means the world to me because we had the best day ever and we were all together. We were all able to just be in the moment as a family."

Tears pricked at the back of my eyes as I finished sharing my most treasured memory. I looked around at all of the unfamiliar faces and a feeling of foolishness worked its way into my body. Why did I decide to share something so personal?

The medium settled her distant eyes on my own as she gently consoled, "Thank you for sharing, Lacy. I do believe that your parents have passed on, but they are both still watching over you and your sister."

My lower lip wobbled as a part of me yearned to believe that our parents were still present in some shape or form. I wanted to believe that their memories and lives hadn't just disappeared into the ground. The finality of death sent a sharp pain into my heart as I grappled with what the older woman had just said.

"Does that mean that the motel isn't haunted?"

"I didn't say that."

Raindrops pelted against the glass window panes as I held a cup of hot chocolate to my chest. The heat soaked into my emotionally exhausted body. I lounged on the third floor away from prying eyes as Evan leaned against an adjacent wall and quietly sipped his black coffee.

The medium had asked to explore the basement and downstairs levels without any interference from the motel owners.

Apparently, the medium wanted to try and speak with the potential spirits in order to see what kept them tethered to the world of the living. Stacy had easily agreed to make herself scarce and scurried into the safety of her room with Jeffrey in tow.

I absently wondered why any self-respecting ghost would bother making an appearance to a camera crew with more than ten men and blinding lights that seemed to rival the sun. The sight of so many people crawling around the motel in search of the supernatural only made the idea of ghosts even more ridiculous and preposterous with every minute that the crew remained.

freshly painted wall.

I bit my tongue and decided against saying something snarky about preserving the integrity of the new paint color on the walls. There was no room for sassy defense mechanisms. Especially, when Evan still looked absolutely ridiculous in suspenders and long knee-high socks. The garments made it difficult for me to take his question seriously, but I gave it my best attempt.

"I'm just curious what they will find besides the stray dust bunny. I'm pretty sure that there isn't anything here."

Evan took a long sip from his cup before he leisurely swallowed and drawled out, "Sure." His tone hinted that he didn't believe any of what I said for even a second.

I groaned and walked over to lean against the opposite wall so that I had a better view of Evan's features. I goaded, "What do you mean?"

Evan shrugged his shoulders and took a longer sip from his cup. How much coffee did he have in there?

about the logic of this situation. When in reality, there is no logic. We were locked downstairs in the basement by an unknown force and just this afternoon I saw a woman walking near your driveway. She definitely wasn't from this time period."

I pursed my lips and chided, "That could have been any member of the television crew. They're all over this place. One of them even asked to see the inside of the shed."

"That's not what I saw. I know it in my bones. You don't need to trust in something outside of your own control, but I do. Lacy, this might have started as a tipsy trick, but it's taken on a life of its own. It's time to admit that you're no longer in control."

I wasn't sure about what part of Evan's speech had managed to touch a nerve, but I was relatively certain that it was the part about giving up control. No way.

A strange thump distracted me from finding a smart rebuttal. At first, it was subtle and quiet enough that I nearly wrote it off as the wind hitting against the window side shutters. However, the noise happened that it sounded like someone was rearranging the items inside of the attic. Odd, I was nearly one hundred percent certain that the entire film crew was downstairs with the medium.

Evan stood to his full height and glanced up at the ceiling. He muttered, "How much do you want to bet that some nosey members of the film crew accidentally locked themselves inside of the attic?"

I laughed, "That poor soul. The attic even gives me the creeps, and I've been up here countless times. The only good thing about that room is the stained-glass window."

"Want to set them free?" Evan tilted his head in the direction of the attic door that was just a few steps further down the hall.

I gave him a devious grin, "Yes, we could use the good karma. They must be so scared. I'm pretty sure that the one lightbulb that's up there burnt out months ago and we still haven't replaced it since it's just so spooky up there."

"Has anything strange ever happened in the attic?" Evan asked.

the hall and indicated with my head to the rope that dangled from the attic entry several feet in the air.

I joked, "Tall people first."

Evan sighed, "Fine. Hold my coffee."

To my surprise, his cup still felt half full. I took a few steps back and watched as Evan effortlessly reached up and gripped the long rope. He quickly gave it a swift yank, but nothing happened.

I bit my lower lip as it curled into my mouth. My entire body wanted to laugh at his clueless confidence. Instead, I brought my cup of hot chocolate closer to my face so that it hovered in front of my mouth and hid my smile as I explained, "You need to unlock the latch first."

There was a brief moment of silence as Evan grunted in agreement and swiftly released the lock. Once he pulled the rope a second time, the scuttle hole opened without further complaint. The folding ladder easily came into view and so did something completely unexpected.

"What's that?" Evan narrowed his eyes as he tried to decipher the outline of the mysterious figure just above the attic stairs. He took a few steps back and nudged me behind his shoulder with every step.

Curious, I peeked out from behind Evan's broad back and laughed. I reached out and flicked on an additional light in the hallway. The light managed to graze the outline of the once ominous figure inside the attic. The previously imposing form quickly shifted into that of a stuffed, plush teddy bear.

"Stacy used to love that bear. It takes up a lot of space and she couldn't throw it away. We compromised and put it in the attic for safekeeping."

Evan slowly nodded his head as he questioned, "Why did you put it so close to the stairs?"

"I didn't and Stacy never went up there." My words evaporated into thin air as we both looked up into the attic and tried to decipher even the smallest, most insignificant flicker of movement. There had to be a reasonable explanation.

it was the main suspect in a murder case instead of a lovable child's toy.

"Yes. Reach into my side pocket. My phone is there." I walked parallel to Evan so that he could more easily grab the phone.

His eyebrows furrowed together until he realized that both of my hands were full of drinks. He nodded his head in understanding and cleared his throat. He gingerly reached into my pocket as his heat radiated close enough so that I could feel his warmth on my own skin.

The moment of odd intimacy ended as Evan retrieved my phone. He opened the phone and used the dim light from the screen to try and see if there was anything else inside of the attic. Seeing as the phone was of no use, I placed the now cool beverages on the hallway side table and swiftly unlocked my bedroom door.

Evan stood guard against the stuffed animal until I returned with an actual battery-powered emergency lantern. I tried to hand the light to Evan, but he sidestepped the offer and kept his eyes glued to the darkness lurking within the attic.

233

After some not very subtle begging and a few vague threats, Evan finally climbed up the ladder. I followed two or three steps behind. Once inside the attic, Evan raised the lantern into the air in an attempt to better illuminate the area.

"Wow, this looks like it could be a bedroom. Look at all of this space. The floor is even finished." Evan tapped on the solid ancient wood flooring for emphasis.

"Yeah. Except for the fact that there is no bathroom and it's super creepy." I placed my hands on my hips as I surveyed the room that spanned the length of the entire downstairs floor plan. Evan was right about the fact that it was massive. I was convinced he was absolutely wrong about the idea of actually using the space as a bedroom. However, he did have a valid point about the finished floors and walls. At one point, it was possible that someone had lived up here.

The space felt oddly sad. I remembered that as a child, I had absolutely hated coming up to the attic to

Now, I looked around and could no longer feel those same strong emotions. The room was colder than the rest of the motel by a few degrees, but I couldn't detect that same amount of sadness or feel an aversion to the space in the same way that I had as a child. Instead, it was as if the memory of the sadness lingered while the actual feeling had completely disappeared from my radar.

"What are you thinking about?"

Evan tilted his head down and inclined it in my direction. He held the lamp out and a few strands of light reflected against the stained-glass window. The only thing that I had ever really enjoyed about the attic.

"Just thinking about how much this place used to give me the creeps, but up here with you, it's not so bad."

Evan joked, "Lacy, you say that now, but we still don't know what was up here making all of that noise. You wouldn't happen to have something up here like a 100-pound cat or a boiler on the blink?"

systems."

The lone light switch made me pause, but then I decided that it was worth a try. I flicked on the switch and to my surprise, the finicky fixture sprung to life. The long-forgotten chairs and extra bedding were all neatly tucked away into the corners of the ample room. A few stray toys from both Stacy's and my own childhood remained neatly placed on the shelves. All except for the plushie that seemed to have walked all the way to the edge of the attic entrance on its own.

Odd.

"I don't know what could have made that noise. The stuffed animal didn't walk away from the other toys. This isn't a Disney movie."

Evan chuckled as he lowered the lamp and walked around the massive area. He looked at all of the ancient items. Some of them I didn't even recognize.

"Hey, Evan."

"Yeah?"

"What if some of these items aren't from my family?"

I rubbed my hands together as a chill settled into my bones. I added, "What if some of these items are from the previous owners of the motel? It's possible that my parents didn't throw everything out when they had first purchased the place."

"What looks unfamiliar?" Evan turned to me as an excited spark burned within his gaze.

I huffed, "A fair amount looks unfamiliar. It's been almost five years since I really bothered to look at the stuff up here. I would be lying if I told you that I could say with certainty what my parents hadn't purchased for the motel. I can estimate some things, but that's honestly about it."

Evan simply shrugged his shoulders and added, "Well, that's a start."

Encouraged by Evan's constantly positive nature, I decided to at least give it a try. I walked deeper into the attic and tried to remember if my parents had ever purchased a random lamp in the shape of a leg or a strange doll that had apparently been defective and instead of eating the pretend food; it had actually eaten

Now that I was thinking about it, I did remember some of the items in a way that people often recalled dreams after waking up. The memories were distant and disjointed, but they were there just enough that they gave me something to grab onto.

I folded my arms around my waist in a gesture partially brought on by the cold, but mostly motivated by warding off all the unintended memories that seemed to bubble to the surface of my consciousness. Each little flicker appeared faster than the last as though my long-lost memories were escaping from a widening crack.

After an unknown amount of time, I slowed down next to a chair. I tried to remember a distant memory linked to the intricately hand-crafted item. Carved rose petals and leaves curved around the legs and back of the chair. It was one of the most detailed items of furniture that I had ever seen.

Evan walked closer once he noticed that I had stopped my inventory of the attic items. He asked, "What is it?"

it's like the sound is on mute. I don't know what she said."

A flicker of frustration gnawed at my chest as I tried to recall more about the memories that I had desperately tried to stomp down into nothing for several years.

"Hey, let me take a look. It seems really old, so that's one clue in our favor."

"Our favor?" I felt like a parrot as I repeated Evan's words.

He quickly explained, "If it's very old, then I doubt that your parents bought it. Most of the motel has an 80s theme from when your parents had first renovated. An old wooden chair doesn't exactly fit that description. Your gut is probably right."

In a brief moment of silence, I listened as the wind outside grew louder. Branches fell in the distance as a deep rumble shook the sky. I suddenly felt like I was in the belly of a giant.

Evan and I locked eyes as the motel shook, completely at the mercy of the weather. Suddenly, a

Panic.

A loud thud quickly rang throughout the suddenly blackened space. I took in a deep gulp of air and tried to process what had just happened.

I muttered, "The lightning probably hit the power lines. We're okay."

My shoulders relaxed as I mentally walked through the possible scenario. A power outage was inconvenient, but definitely not supernatural or dangerous if we remained safely inside of the motel.

However, panicked heavy breathing told me that Evan likely did not come to the same conclusion. I called out, "Evan?"

Harsh breathing sounded from somewhere in the distance. I wasn't exactly sure what had happened, but I knew that Evan needed a little help.

"Evan? Are you okay? Talk to me so that I can follow your voice."

A shaky voice answered, "It's closed."

Confused, I stuck out a hand in front of my face. I felt like I was tumbling down the looking glass after so to find a moment of clarity when navigating a ship through fog.

I sighed as the light from the stained-glass window and chaotic thunderous storm slowly melted away. A thick darkness clung around my arms, but I kept moving. Suddenly, I was too far into the room for any light to reach me.

I called out, "What do you mean? What's closed?"

Evan's uneven breathing sounded closer than before as I took another tentative step in what I hoped was his direction.

"Evan, you need to call out so that I can get to you. I can tell that you're scared, so let me find you because I'm scared too. I'd rather be scared together instead of being scared alone." The admission easily slid from my tongue as I bravely took another blind step into the unknown. In the back of my mind, I hoped that I wasn't anywhere near the attic door. The last thing that I wanted was to fall through to the third floor.

After a brief pause, an uneven voice called, "I'm here, Lacey. I'm next to the attic door. It's slammed shut.

family's pantry as a kid. The lock was childproof, so when I tried to get some more cereal, I ended up wedged inside. It took my mom hours to find me. I really don't like small dark spaces, Lacy."

I listened intently to Evan's every word. The sincerity that tinged his voice pulled at my heart. I wished that I had been there to help get a much younger Evan out of the pesky pantry. It sounded horrifying.

In the back of my mind, I registered that someone had apparently locked us inside of the attic, but I decided to deal with that detail after finding Evan. I wondered what had happened to make the lamp suddenly stop working. I knew that I had replaced the batteries at the end of the summer and had only used them once to find pruning scissors inside of the gardening shed. By all accounts, the lamp should still be able to work.

Just a few more steps. I followed Evan's voice as he spoke and I extended my arm a little more in the darkness in order to reach him.

Suddenly, I bumped into something solid and knew that it was Evan from the way that he grumbled a to the ground.

"Thanks for finding me, Lacy. Took you long enough." Evan's voice held a hint more certainty than before.

"Well, it's my first time trying to find an entire person in the dark. I thought it turned out okay for my first try. Here, take my hand."

Evan asked, "Where are we going?"

I wrapped my fingers around Evan's hand and said, "Follow the light."

"You just had to say that in a situation where ghosts just locked us inside an attic."

"See, I knew that you would get the pun."

Lightning reflected from the stained-glass window and hues of red and blue danced around the attic. The round window was about a few feet wide and it was just large enough so that Evan and I could comfortably sit down on the ancient wooden floor and still look out at the windy storm-torn property.

A loud roar suddenly shook the motel and I quickly reached out and gripped Evan's wrist as the floorboards creaked and groaned in protest.

"What was that?"

Evan narrowed his eyes as he looked out the window and answered, "It sounds like lightning probably struck the fireplace."

The news of lightning felt a little too close for comfort as I pursed my lips in dismay. I had no interest in getting accidentally electrocuted.

I couldn't decide which one was worse between the increasingly haunting behavior and the obviously escalating storm.

The colors from the lightning were faint as they passed through the stained-glass and ghosted against the attic? I was relatively sure that Stacy would come looking if I wasn't around by the morning. Stacy knows how much I value getting work done early in the morning, so hopefully, she'll get worried if I'm a no show.

I stretched out my leg as pins and needles began to poke around at the top of my thigh. I accidentally nudged Evan's leg, but he didn't seem to mind. In fact, the gentle nudge seemed to bring him away from his own thoughts.

In the dim light of the storm, I could barely decipher his features. I knew that he disliked being stuck in the dark, but something in his expression bordered on panic. His eyes stared into the distance and his jaw looked so tense that I wondered if he would accidentally chip a tooth with so much pressure.

Eventually, Evan felt my worried gaze and he managed to pull his eyes out of a realm that I couldn't follow. His eyes raged with an odd passion that I didn't understand, but something deep within my gut told me that whatever was on his mind wasn't going to be good.

deep within his joints. He looked like a man about to walk the plank. A man about to meet his judge, jury, and executioner. Evan looked terrified.

He painstakingly fixed one of his suspenders as it had managed to slide down his shoulder.

A small snort escaped my nose as I looked at Evan's outfit. I sidestepped the question in his gaze and said, "You didn't need to wear that for me."

Evan's features turned subdued as he solemnly answered, "Yes, I did."

The sound was faint and whispered into the room like a gentle breeze against the branches of a tree.

I looked Evan deep in his soulful eyes as I finally mustered the courage to ask the question that had been whirling around the back of my mind all night.

"Why?"

The storm outside seemed to intensify with every passing second. Wind howled louder than a banshee as rain furiously pounded against the newly replaced roof shingles.

I wanted Evan to spill his guts in an organized list, but all I received was a long and extended silence. His features looked agonized and I wanted him to spit it out.

Finally, Evan muttered, "I need you to understand that I never wanted to hurt you."

Immediately, I straightened my posture and grew more rigid as I waited for Evan to break open the dam. I tried to reason that whatever Evan said couldn't possibly be that bad. He only had the best intentions when it came to the motel and my family. Maybe Evan had accidentally broken the lamp? The guess was a shot in the dark, but it was still better than nothing. All that Evan had managed to do so far was give me a case of indigestion.

Impatient and unsettled, I prodded, "Evan, tell me."

He explained, "Growing up, I was a really difficult kid. My dad was out of the picture by the time that I turned twelve. I started hanging out with the older kids from a rougher area of town and got into trouble. My mom was desperate, but nothing she did or said ever connected with me. I was angry and didn't know how to put it into words. One day, I came up the hill and began spraying graffiti on the back of the shed just for something to do. I don't even remember I was drawing in the spray paint. Something pointless. Your dad came out and very calmly laid out a deal. He said that I could work around the outside of the motel for the summer and fix the graffiti and in return, he wouldn't go to the cops or tell my mom. Over the course of the summer, I saw you with your sister maybe once or twice. It was that summer when you and Stacy were both busy with swim camp at the public pool, so you two were rarely around. At first, I was bitter and often gave your dad a hard time mowing the lawn or painting over the graffiti. It took four different coats of paint before the graffiti finally decided to stay hidden. Eventually, I started to see him as an adult that I could respect and turn to for advice. I asked business. He gave me the opportunity to not only have a business but to potentially have a really good and happy life."

Tears freely fell down my face as I listened to every word that Evan said in complete shock. Impossible.

How could I possibly forget someone that looked like Evan even when we were children? I winced at the realization that I had actively pushed down and suppressed so much of my childhood. It was possible that Evan had been part of that timeline and I had purposely ignored his presence in my past.

Still, I asked, "But I don't remember you. I'm sure that if you worked outside of the motel for an entire summer that I'd remember you."

Evan gave a dry chuckle as he added, "I was relatively well-fed at that point in my life. I really had a thing for fast food and a strong hatred for working out."

"I guess that explains why you prefer Veggiefresh Promise pizza to the greasier competition." I made a half-hearted joke that turned rather flat on delivery, but Evan was able to understand.

not even close to the center of my life, but they're definitely in the background."

Evan added, "Your dad was the one that taught me the value of hard work and the importance of putting in a little elbow grease."

He always told me, "Evan, nothing is more important than a little elbow grease and faith."

"Faith." I finished Evan's sentence and my eyes instantly widened with the realization that he really had known my dad. Emotions swirled around like a tornado as I desperately grappled to understand what Evan had just told me. The entire situation just felt so impossibly improbable, but then again we were possibly trapped together in an attic because of ghosts. So, anything was possible.

Eventually, I prodded, "Why didn't you say anything?"

For a minute, Evan simply sucked his lips over his teeth. The action made his face look like he had just tasted something extremely bitter. His lips slowly returned from the depths of his mouth and he sighed.

"Lacey, it was pretty obvious that you hate

you to write me out of your life before even giving me a chance. We started getting to know each other and telling you just grew harder and harder. I wanted to tell you when there was a good time, but it never seemed right. Honestly, a big part of me was scared that if I told you then you wouldn't want anything to do with me. That wasn't fair of me and I'm sorry. I didn't want you to think that I wanted to get to know you out of pity."

I mustered the most venom that I could find within my wobbly voice and angrily hissed, "Pity."

The single word burned the back of my throat as if it was made from acid. It seared my insides and heated my previously freezing skin. Of all the people in town, Evan was the last person that I had ever wanted to receive pity from.

I mulled over Evan's words and had to agree that what he was saying made sense. Most of the time, I often avoided interaction with any old friends of my parents. Heck, I still hadn't been able to go inside of the town diner because it just felt too overwhelming.

Slowly, a deep rage settled into my chest. I decided to cling to that feeling instead of the sadness or and I pulled my legs up closer to my chest and actively avoided touching Evan.

The message was clear. Evan flinched back as if he had been slapped. We sat in silence as the storm outside made enough noise for both of us combined.

I didn't want to look at Evan. He had put everything on the table and allowed me the opportunity to judge his actions. Now, I needed a minute to think about everything before I accidentally said anything stupid.

Anger and a convoluted sadness remained constant in my body. How could he keep such a secret? What kind of memories did he have with my father? Did my dad teach Evan about cars? Hundreds of questions kept repeating on a never-ending loop and I felt like I had been plucked from the ground and tossed into a tornado of raging, disjointed thoughts and emotions.

A strange sense of vulnerability crept around my chest. I felt ridiculous. For months, Evan had been so kind and now maybe all of that kindness and affection was just misplaced guilt and grief for my father. What if what Evan really felt for me wasn't a small blossom of hole.

Evan and I sat mere inches away from each other, but the distance could have been that of the Grand Canyon. Neither of us managed to say another word as the rain gradually lessened to a gentle sprinkle.

Eventually, several voices murmured from the floor below. I glanced out the window and noticed the faintest signs of sunlight as hues of pink and yellow danced along the horizon. We had spent the entire night trapped inside of the stuffy attic with little to show for our adventure except for a few stray tears and an Earth-shattering admission.

Banging from below hinted at the arrival of reinforcements. Suddenly, the attic door swung down and eager steps quickly jaunted up the ladder.

Bright curious eyes framed by glossy hair looked between my exhausted face and Evan's blank stare. Stacy looked at us completely puzzled as she asked, "What are you two doing locked in the attic?"

I placed my cold hands on the tops of my knees as I pushed my body into a standing position. I

My feet walked straight to the attic stairs without sparing Evan a second glance. Every cell within my body screamed for freedom. I didn't want to spend another second with the man that had lied about his identity the entire time that we had known each other.

Stacy gave Evan a confused glance as I quickly scampered down the stairs as if the attic was on fire. Evan's usually upbeat demeanor was replaced by a dark cloud as he nodded in acknowledgement to Stacy and then quickly made a beeline down the stairs. He headed down the hallway and then descended the spiral staircase. I assumed that Evan was headed to the front door of the motel and didn't bother to stop him.

"What happened up there?" Stacy wiggled her nose and glanced at Jeffrey as he swiftly shut and relocked the attic door.

I didn't bother to stop and explain. Instead, I retreated to the safety of my bedroom. Once there, I slammed my bedroom door shut a little harder than necessary.

I really hoped that some time to think would help clear my mind. The exhaustion coupled with the painful and uncomfortable situations that I'd be stuck in the same pattern for the rest of my life.

It had been three days since the camera crew had left the motel. The crew hadn't captured any concrete evidence of the paranormal, but every member of the team had expressed a strong interest in never returning to the motel again. Even the woman that had spoken to me earlier about visiting with her family now seemed apprehensive about such an idea. The possibility of the potential ghosts and ghouls now felt too probable to ignore. Luckily, only the furniture seemed to move around at will as the storm had managed to set everyone on edge and done the rest.

A storm that had only occurred on the very top of the hill. Apparently, the rest of the town hadn't experienced even a light mist that fateful night. It was as if the motel had conjured its very own weather pattern.

I hadn't spoken to Evan since we had escaped from the attic. For days, I typed out several lengthy email drafts on my computer, but none of them had sounded right. Each draft sounded less and less angry and more and more hurt. In all honesty, I really wanted to know if Evan had decided to stay around for me or out managed to come out the right way. Heck, I had managed to avoid going to town for three days under the thinly-veiled guise of exhaustion.

If Stacy knew anything different, she had simply agreed and headed off into town for the motel chores. It appeared that luck was on my side.

My thoughts jumped from one scenario to another as snow and watered-down slush crunched under the weight of feet only a few paces away. I wrestled with a few fallen branches in the yard as I waited for Stacy to approach. The storm had most definitely done a number on the property and I still hadn't fully inspected the motel for damage.

Stacy came into view with two cups of steaming hot chocolate and a cherry red blanket draped over her slim birdlike shoulders. She held out one cup like a strategic peace offering and asked, "Can we talk?"

So much for being lucky, I thought miserably.

"Now, before you start raising your hackles and hissing, just promise to hear me out." Stacy held the cup in a death grip as I reached out for the handle.

I arched an eyebrow, but quickly nodded in agreement. I didn't want the little marshmallows to disappear before I was able to get the first sip. Besides, I knew that Stacy would just pester me about whatever was on her mind at a different time if I didn't agree to listen now. At least now, there was hot chocolate with mini marshmallows. A bribe that I was willing to begrudgingly accept.

Hot chocolate in hand, I took a cautionary sip. It tasted delicious and I noticed that Stacy had even added extra marshmallows to the cup. A trick that she only used when she really wanted something.

"Okay, Stacy. You've bribed me. What's on your mind?"

"Lacy, talk to me about Evan."

Nope.

I took a step back and looked around the slosh-covered grass as if it held all the answers in the

Stacy snapped, "Lacy! Please, you have to let someone in to talk about these things. Let's talk it over and see if there is anything that can be done. These past few months, you have been so happy. I haven't seen you that happy or carefree since university. If there is even the smallest chance that I can help make you happy then please let me try. You always do everything to make sure that Jeffrey and I have everything that we need. Let me return the favor. I really want to be that person for you. Please, give me the chance."

It felt as if rocks had settled at the bottom of my belly. I had never known that keeping a stiff upper lip meant that Stacy had felt distant and isolated from me.

"I'm sorry, Stacy. I didn't know. I never wanted to make you feel like I was keeping you out of my life. Everything just felt so overwhelming with mom and dad and the motel. I didn't want to add my stress to yours. I figured that it would be easier to keep it to myself. I just felt like all I've been doing is treading water instead of actually trying to swim."

"What about me?" Stacy whispered.

simple question.

Stacy continued, "It's been hard for me, too. I'm lucky that I can talk with Jeffrey about stuff, but it's not the same. I miss talking about important things with my sister. You need to talk with me and you need to talk with people who were friends with our parents. We're a group of people that want to help, but how can we help if you avoid us or don't want to let us in?"

I lowered the cup and defensively quipped, "I don't mind telling you what's on my mind, but I won't share with the people from town. Not the people that were friends with mom and dad."

For a split second, the image of Evan's goofy smiling face as he donned a powdered wig and wore suspenders came to mind. He had apparently been a good friend of our father. The image opened an emotional can of worms.

"What?" Stacy asked, as she noticed the slight frown that pulled at the edges of my mouth.

I drew in a deep breath and explained, "Evan said that he knew dad. He said that dad had helped him to start his garage."

263

can't believe that I couldn't see the resemblance."

I frowned, "How can you remember that?"

Stacy laughed, "It's not easy to forget a kid that's barely taller than five feet trying to mow our massive front lawn. He looked like he was wrestling with the weeds. I thought it was hilarious. It makes sense that dad kept in touch with Evan over the years. Dad had a soft spot for the kid. Evan definitely grew into his looks, but don't we all?"

The added tidbit of information helped to settle some of my misgivings. Hearing Stacy vouch that Evan had helped around the motel as a child, managed to soothe some of the worries. Maybe I simply felt unsettled because, at the end of the day, I was more than sure that the unease came from trying to be more vulnerable. After all, it just wasn't something on my usual agenda.

"Lacy, it's not the end of the world. He told you that he knew dad, right?"

I smacked my lips together in disdain and the sound reverberated from my lips and quickly dissolved into the open yard. "Right."

asked, "So, what's the problem?"

That was the million-dollar question. What was the problem? The question had managed to elude me for days.

The truth sounded silly once I finally managed to understand why I felt so upset. Eventually, I mumbled in a tone of false nonchalance, "It sounds silly to say it out loud."

Stacy rolled her eyes, "If you are feeling a strong emotion, then it's clearly not silly. Emotions aren't silly. They're part of who we are and help us to piece together our lives. Spill."

"Fine, but don't say I didn't warn you. I am afraid that Evan only wanted to hang around the motel because he felt a duty to dad. I mean, the motel was one or two more bad bills from ruin when we first met Evan. It really needed help. What if he's only sticking around because of dad? What if…"

I abruptly ended my last sentence. I quickly ended it with a tone of finality, but one glance at Stacy told me that wasn't allowed. I licked my lower lip and tried again, "What if Evan wasn't really interested in

The moment of vulnerability made me feel like I needed to find the nearest rock and hide. I quickly added, "It's silly, just like I said."

Stacy took a long sip of her chocolate drink as she weighed my words. Eventually, Stacy said, "Not silly. Maybe the best thing that you can do is to just ask him. If you keep your distance, then you'll never really know the truth. You'll just know the made-up version of the truth that's in your mind and fits with what you believe. Asking for his truth might be hard, but it's better than never knowing. Don't you agree?"

Dang it. Since when did Stacy get so smart?

I sighed, "There's just one more thing that I still have trouble figuring out."

Stacy tilted her head to the side and asked, "Like what?"

"How did you end up being the younger sister?"

I clutched a small clipboard and slowly walked around the perimeter of the motel. I just needed to make sure that everything was in order before heading into town to talk with Evan.

The impending task meant that I was in no rush to quickly finish the inspection since it was the only thing standing between me and spilling my guts to Evan.

I turned the corner and noticed a few odd burn marks on the ground. It looked like lightning had constantly struck around one particular area of the motel. The soggy grass and rose bushes that framed the side of the house contained small burn patches that looked similar to massive cigarette burns rubbed into the ground. How had the rest of the town managed to avoid such a dangerous storm?

My curious gaze eventually traveled to the actual side of the motel. Within seconds, I found my heart lodged in the side of my throat. What had happened to the chimney?

Bricks were scattered around the rose bushes like feathers from a downed bird. I imagined that the lightning had behaved like a nefarious stray cat and had abused the chimney within an inch of its life before getting bored and moving on to its next potential prey.

I sighed and walked over to inspect the damage. A hole in the chimney stood about level with my head. Upon closer inspection, I wasn't exactly sure what to make of the damage. A metallic circular tube remained hidden deep inside of the rubble. I tried to think of any reason for the presence of the tube, but came up short. The chimney was only wood-burning seeing as my parents had never bothered to convert it to use gas.

"If you're not a gas pipeline, then what are you?" The question stood unanswered in the breeze as I reached out a hand and gingerly tugged on the cool metal.

To my surprise, the item easily pulled away from the rest of the chimney as dust and brick fragments fell down into the charred soil like flakes of ash. I used the back of my sleeve and wiped down the pesky tube. The

One end of the tube looked less solid than the other, so I decided to try and unscrew it. I figured that it was worth a try in order to have at least one working clue about the motel. The blasted item seemed determined to stay shut. I carefully turned it around in my hands. Suddenly, I noticed the smallest keyhole.

"Bingo."

I reached into my shirt and quickly plucked out the small key that I had diligently carried around for weeks in the faintest hopes of running into this exact moment.

The small key looked like an exact match to the petite divot in the metallic cylinder. I mumbled, "Only one way to find out."

The top effortlessly popped off and then clattered around in the mud-covered ground. I was too focussed on the contents within the cylinder to care. The ends of a piece of paper protruded from the opening and I gingerly pinched the material between my thumb and index finger as I painstakingly pulled it out. The entire scene made me feel somewhat like an archeologist uncovering long forgotten secrets. However, these tales and secrets were literally hidden within the walls of my home.

With as much care as possible, I unraveled the paper and scanned the handwritten content. The stack contained several pages and I could barely keep calm enough to try and decipher the scrawling penmanship.

I tried to read it out loud in order to put the pieces together, "John, you have always had my heart. It was you from the very first moment in town when our eyes connected. I don't want to marry a different man and spend the rest of my life living a filthy lie. Father wants a marriage that will benefit him and the paper. He refuses to have any compassion on the subject of my future happiness. I regret not running away with you last not writing that dreadful story that he had requested of you. We both know that it was a lie. The mayor never hurt his wife and the article was only intended to ruin the man's career. You did the right thing by standing on the side of truth and please never regret that for a moment. The fact that my father is such a vengeful man that he would try to keep us separated as punishment, is a most cruel and unusual torture. Your integrity is part of the reason that my heart remains yours. He might try to manipulate the good hearts and unsuspecting minds of the people in this town to spite you, but my heart will always embrace you for understanding the importance of integrity. Have faith that the truth always comes to light and will surely set us free. John, remain true and righteous in your convictions as we face these dark times together. I plan to run from the house tonight and I will remain hidden at our spot in the woods until you are able to join. The snow should hide my tracks from sight and allow me to reach our spot undetected. The hounds are away from the house this week so it is my only chance of finding freedom and a future. I am sure that you will find this message as it's tucked right underneath the

I read the entire letter twice in my head after reading it out loud. What did this letter mean? Why would Lilian be reported missing if she ran away with the man that she loved? Suddenly, I remembered that John had been blamed in the newspaper articles in the library as a villainous man connected to Lilian's disappearance.

"The paper. Lilian's father controlled the town newspaper. No wonder he made sure to ruin John's name."

I carefully looked at the next page and realized that it was a neatly folded excerpt from the newspaper. The crease lines of the folded paper had worn away the words stuck within the folds. The story was important enough that Lilian had bothered to stuff it into the metallic canister with her carefully crafted letter to the love of her life.

Mayor Leads Life of Scandal. Leaves Town to Mayor Elect and Soon-To-Be Son-in-Law of Mr. Lockwood.

This scandal comes less than a week after the old town Mayor had hosted a town hall assembly on the importance of virtue and morality. The content obviously fell on his own deaf ears as he is now wanted for charges of immorality. Defamed Mayor Jiff Boone is the town's newest outlaw and is often found consorting in saloons late at night with other shady characters such as the once reputable John O'Ceallaigh. No charges or proof of wrongdoing have been brought against John O'Ceallaigh, the former editor-in-chief of this paper, but many townspeople believe charges are pending.

If you see the sullied Mayor Jiff Boone report his location to the paper or new Sheriff, immediately. Claim a potentially generous award provided by our dedicated leader and patron, Mr. Lockwood.

"Lilian's father was so vile. No wonder poor Lilian decided to escape." I muttered the words under my breath as I finished reading the newspaper clipping.

A chill ran down my spine that had nothing to do with hiding underneath the slight overhang of the roof near several inches of mud and damp Earth. This frigid feeling had everything to do with how poor Lilian had waited until the last minute to take back control of her life.

If Lilian had been successful then why had all of the papers written about John being wanted for her disappearance?

The date in the corner of the clipping had faded and smudged with age, but I was willing to bet my last dollar that it predated the fire in the library by several decades. I absently plopped the metal canister against my hip as my eyes scanned the ancient documents that were gingerly grasped in my other hand.

A dull rattle told me that the canister wasn't as empty as I had thought. I placed the palm of my hand over the top of the tube and flipped it upside down. A arms and quickly realized that it was another key.

My eyes lit up with childlike excitement. For once, I knew exactly what needed to be done. I painstakingly refolded the papers along the original creases and returned them back to the tube.

Once satisfied, I could no longer contain my excitement as I sped back inside of the motel. My footsteps pounded up the main stairway with all of the grace of an elephant as I made a beeline for the mysterious box that I had plucked from the library so many weeks ago.

Today, I was getting an answer.

A heavy wheeze escaped my chest as I frantically ascended the final step. I clutched the metal tube to my chest and stumbled down the hallway. It was the first time in my entire life where the hallway had ever felt so long.

Usually, the hallway seemed much too short as Jeffrey and Stacy often made it very clear during the night. However, those old thoughts felt like distant memories as I tried my best to breathe through a painful cramp in my side. Had I always been this out of shape or was this new?

Doesn't matter.

I swiftly opened my bedroom door and it swung back into the wall with a firm thud. I felt like a woman possessed by my own self-assigned mission. My fingers reached out and grabbed the other heavy metallic box between my fingers that momentarily managed to resemble something closer to talons.

I felt like a creature that had escaped from a Tolkien novel as I desperately clutched both metal boxers to my chest.

to make the walls vibrate as if their quiet lips were dying to speak and tell the first living soul about a mystery that had led to heartache and suspicion for over 100 years.

Mud covered shoes flew across the room as I hastily kicked them off and gently placed the two metallic objects in the middle of my well-used slightly torn bedspread. I decided that my personal rule about not wearing outside clothes on my bed could be slightly bent just this one. After all, it was in the name of love and mystery.

"Now what do you have in here? What is so special that Lilian had felt the need to store it underneath the library?" I touched the box with a newfound sense of reverence. My fingers hummed with a strange mix of nervousness and electricity. The anticipation made my fingers shake as I retrieved the newly discovered key and brought it closer to the lock. My hands shook and missed the lock, but on the third try my unsteady fingers finally managed to hit the mark.

The box groaned in protest as it opened for the very first time in decades. I opened the box as wide as possible and gasped at what I found.

A small curved glass orb regally sat in the middle of the red velvet lined interior of the box. Inside of the box, there was also a small piece of paper with an obviously handwritten note. It wasn't more than three lines long.

I traced my fingers along the curved glass and wondered why such an odd object had meant so much to Lilian. Carefully, I picked it up and realized that the bottom had been deeply pressed into the velvet and hidden from sight. It wasn't a glass orb, but a very finely decorated snow-globe.

The silver base shone even in the faint light from the half-opened curtains as little particles of dust swirled around in the air. Inside of the globe, stood a miniature sized version of the motel. It took a moment for me to recognize it as the color was different from today, but it was definitely the motel from a time back when it had still been called a home.

An inscription near the base caught my gaze as I read, "John, may we one day turn this large house into a home. I pray we have the courage to try."

John. It had sat for decades unloved and unknown within a dark dank library basement. I made a mental note to find out what had happened to John and his family even though the old newspapers had made it very obvious that he had been blamed and likely imprisoned for Lilian's disappearance if he hadn't already disappeared.

"How could something so romantic backfire so tragically?"

The words no sooner left my lips before a feeling of deep dread washed over me. Was it possible that Lilian was the ghostly woman that I had noticed in the hallway?

The night that the medium had arrived at the motel, only Evan and I had managed to actually see Lilian. Everyone else had felt the presence of something else, but hadn't managed to see an actual figure.

A light bulb suddenly turned on in my mind. Lilian had never made it to her hiding spot with John. That's why Evan had found her ghost wandering in men's clothing near the front of the property. It was very likely that she had frozen to death in the extreme temperatures and the snow had covered her tracks so that what had happened to the woman that he had loved.

I gently shook the snow-globe and watched completely mesmerized as little flakes of imaginary snow fell onto the motel. The scene felt surreal and a tad ironic. Lilian had unknowingly gifted Jack with the map to her final resting place.

"This is too dark." I placed the snow-globe back in the velvet lined box and then gingerly picked up the note that I had ignored earlier in favor of exploring the intricately crafted orb.

The words were minimal, but I read each word out loud in a desperate hope that maybe Lilian had managed to meet Jack. I took in a deep gulp of air and read, "Jack, I was scared to leave with you, but that fear was misplaced. I now know life is intended to be lived with the ones that we love by our side. No matter how perilous the first steps may be. I just hope that I'm not too late."

Upset, I paced around the confines of my bedroom. Lilian deserved better, but her plan had absolutely failed and Jack never knew where to find her.

walked over and realized that it was Evan's jacket. He had taken it off the night that the film crew had arrived and had rushed out of the front door before he had retrieved it.

I didn't have the heart to throw it out or return it so it had sat in the corner of my room like a low budget vigil. I really did miss him.

The material still held Evans' woodsy masculine scent as if it had permanently melded into the fibers of the jacket. Slowly, I looked between the snow-globe and jacket.

A small smile crept along the edges of my lips as I whispered out into the seemingly empty room, "You win, Lilian."

Fifteen minutes had never felt so perilous. I wiped the sweat from my palms onto the nicest pair of jeans that I owned. After a few minutes, I parked the truck and watched as several mechanics worked over multiple cars as they casually chatted to one another with coffee. It looked like a friendly garage that took great pride in their work.

"Makes sense." I snickered. Of course, Evan owned the most productive and friendly garage in town. I opened the car door and hopped out of the truck. The jump from the seat to the ground somehow felt farther than usual as I gripped Evan's jacket in one hand and unceremoniously slapped the ground with the other.

For a moment, I sat on the concrete floor with my mouth hanging open like a gasping fish. What had just happened? Mechanics from the garage bustled over as I remained as frozen to the ground as the patch of black ice that I had slipped on. Concerned faces covered in grease popped around my field of vision.

"What's going on out here? Did you guys finally befriend that stray dog?" Evan's voice cut through the

His curious gaze landed on my splayed figure as my cheeks turned an even darker shade of red. Eventually, I composed myself enough so that I simply sat on the floor and offered Evan his jacket.

Evan frowned as he looked between the jacket and me. He called to the curious onlookers, "Okay, thanks for the concern, guys. You can head back to the garage."

He reached out his hands and instead offered to pull me up. I accepted the offer and practically flew back onto my feet as Evan effortlessly placed me back on the ground.

"Thanks for the help."

Evan replied, "Thanks for the jacket."

There was a momentary pause before Evan gripped the jacket between both of his hands and drawled, "That's an inconvenient drive just for a jacket."

I gratefully accepted the nudge, "Maybe I came for more than just a jacket. Do you want to grab some food at the diner?"

"Sure. You know that means we will run into the lunch crowd regulars, right?"

show my face."

Evan's thick eyebrows practically disappeared into his hairline at the response. He gauged the look on my face for a moment and then asked, "Why?"

"Let's just say that I don't want to repeat the mistakes of the past."

"Will you tell me more about that decision over lunch?" Evan shuffled his feet as he tilted his head to the side and waited for me to reply.

I smiled, "Absolutely. You drive."

"Deal."

We headed over to Evan's car as curious stares from the garage followed our every move.

"I take it you don't get many visitors."

Evan chuckled, "You're the first, but you should come around more often. It will help lessen the shock factor for them if they see you around the garage more frequently."

"I can do that."

"Good. Let's eat."

with the menu."

"Take your time, Lacy. Some of the lunch items have changed, but the menu is mostly the same."

"Isn't that the truth."

I wasn't exactly thinking of just the menu as I responded. It seemed that the history of the town was oddly similar to the menu. The more that the people and places changed, the more that the actual story stayed the same. This time, I knew how to change the ending of this particular story.

The End?

California native, Camille Cabrera writes suspense and mystery novels that focus on a specific holiday. She loves to mix reality with fiction in order to create the perfect enthralling story. She adores her two cats and enjoys collecting various stickers and stamps from around the world. When not being old before her time, Camille can be found writing her next novel in a random be the author of this book.

You can visit her website: **www.CamilleCabrera.com**

Check out:

Catalina's Tide

Seven friends set out on a Fourth of July vacation that soon becomes sinister. Paranoia in the group runs high after they hear about the successful cloning of Dolly the Sheep. But is 1996 the first time an animal has been successfully cloned or the first time that the public finds out about the success of cloning? Friendships are tested and motives come into question when a member of the group begins to act differently after adventuring on the island. The situation of once unfounded paranoia spirals into actual terror when people start to go missing.

When it's almost the millennium... reality is scarier than science fiction.

Perfect for readers interested in 90 minutes short thriller, suspense, and science fiction stories.